I0537835

# CONTENTS

## Forward

The most dangerous animal on planet Earth is human. In 2021 there are more soldiers and former soldiers with special killer skillsets than at any time since the Second World War.

**ISBN:** 978-1-7398822-0-4

## About the Author

Born in Africa in the early '50s settled in London in the late '50s. Later moved and settled in Northern Ireland with his wife four children dog, cat, and goat. Now retired from public service and writing because he enjoys it. Interested in various genres including crime, humour, political satire, paranormal, science-fiction and, westerns. Hence his work covers a broad range of topics. Loves animals, classic cars, old movies and fish and chips.

# Table of Content

# CHAPTER ONE

## How it begins

A man betrayed by his own people is the most dangerous animal on our planet. Worse still if trained as a soldier. Military personnel follow codes break them and you remove all restraints. Leaving their limitations to their own imagination about how to use their highly trained skill set to wreak havoc on those who wronged them. Those who should have known better.

On the day of his release from prison Leo Priest guessed that his enemies were aware that he had finally been freed. Fifteen years of his life wasted unfairly for something he did not do. Most in his position would have focused on revenge and to be honest, he couldn't argue it hadn't crossed his mind

But fifteen years was a long time to mellow. A long time to plan for a future that should have begun all those years ago. They say the older you get the wiser you get. Maybe that's what happened. Maybe he just needed to forget the past and focus on the future. Maybe?

Thing was there remained a piece of him that held doubt. A piece that urged he not let the bastard get away with it. Of course it would probably be suicide if he did choose to find the one responsible, but if the idea of dying while making the attempt should have acted as a deterrent. It didn't.

His spell in the British army had cured him of worrying about dying. Combat tours around the globe tend to do that. Your life always on the line until it isn't. That's when you're dead. So, you live for the moment. In prison, at least went he first arrived it felt much the same until he squared things with the other inmates. Demonstrating that it would take several to bring him down if they got lucky. A few made the attempt and lost big time. After that there were no more distractions. He had taken great care not to kill anyone. A few broken bones had gotten who he was over to even the toughest among them and he still got to leave prison after fifteen years.

Joining the British army at sixteen life had taken a turn for the better. Living with a father more interested in a whiskey bottle than his son had almost robbed him of the will to live. The army provided a kind of family he had been missing since his mother walked out when he was aged twelve. She remained just a memory since then as she had never made the effort to see him again. He wasn't sure how he was meant to feel about her lack of interest. For a while he felt angry, then later he guessed it was for the best. Nowadays, he had no feelings one way or the other.

In 1992 when he enlisted, the issues facing the British army were fewer than today and resources more plentiful. However, signs that peace was destabilising around the globe, especially in the Middle East were emerging. But it was Europe that introduced him to modern warfare after the Bosnian War kicked off. Deployed among the British contingent with NATO forces, realisation that his young life could easily be shortened occurred suddenly when his platoon sergeant took a bullet to the head directly in front of him. They were patrolling a forest track. Trees either side with a bend just ahead. Overhead a bright Sun in an empty blue sky. Only the trees blocking it out as they made slow progress.

Self-survival abruptly all too real as the training he received automatically triggered actions. Hitting the dirt, keeping his chinclose to stones and earth while scanning ahead for gun flashes. Around him people shouted but too indistinct to be understood. Rolling a couple of times to the right put him behind a tall tree masked by green foliage. The perfect blanket as he rolled further into the forest over leaves, broken twigs, and a rabbit hole without attracting attention. Crawling on his stomach made for slow progress while gunfire repeatedly echoed all around followed by cries from comrades. Going forward or back to help others created a momentary dilemma. Moving forward his choice. Killing the enemy his intention. He couldn't guess how long he had been moving. Possibly an eternity but in reality barely minutes. Ahead of him he spotted gun flashes as a sniper fired again. It was odd he thought moving slowly, carefully while trying to avoid making any sound. He imagined he should be scared. Enough veterans had warned him including his platoon sergeant. Adding that there was no humiliation for a sixteen-year-old to be scared. Fear was a shared experience in combat. Only those passed caring remained unmoved. Maybe he was dead? The thought shot through his head faster than any bullet. If he was dead then why was the ground still being tough on his belly? Besides, he thought, not being scared meant he would be steady when the time came to take the shot to silence the sniper.

With a sigh that pushed all other thoughts aside he continued. Excited and tense like a taut spring. His finger hovering over the trigger ready to snap it back the moment a threat appeared. Another shot rang out the long muzzle of a rifle suddenly clear between the leaves ahead and above him. Moving at a snail's pace he crawled behind a thick tree trunk and lifted himself off the ground. For the first time he heard the artificial silence all around broken only by the wailing of wounded somewhere behind. No birds or animal sounds. No breeze. Nothing. An intense brooding stillness expectant for another death.

He swallowed. The sound loud in his ears. He hoped the sniper hadn't heard. Closing his eyes he imagined where the sniper was hidden gauging where he needed to point his own weapon. He likely had one chance. A miss would make his death probable. Another flitting thought entered his head what was the age of his enemy? Older than sixteen? Was he a virgin? Dumb questions but he was thinking them.

His thoughts dissipated as he stepped out from behind the trunk and fired. A single bullet. All that was required. His enemy fell from the tree striking the ground with a heavy thud. He stared at the body. Slow to move, he finally stepped forward and stared down at the face of a bearded middle-aged man in a military uniform. Someone's father? His first kill. The first time never leaves you. Like your first love. A milestone in anyone's life.

In 1999 again as part of a NATO taskforce he found himself engaged in combat and peacekeeping operations in Kosovo. A year later he was on the African continent in Sierra Leone involved supporting government forces in another Civil War. His combat operations ended after deployment to Afghanistan as a twenty-five-year-old sergeant with ten years combat experience and medals to prove it. Two tours later he found himself seconded to the Military/Civil Police Co-operation Unit (MCPCU) based in the U.K. A gesture by the army to allow him a break from combat.

Protecting people instead of killing them was a welcome change, and not as different as expected. Reverse role play from experience gained in combat zones using a killers instincts was expected to defend against client injury or premature death.

It was good to be out of prison he thought as his mind returned to the present. Looking up at a cloudy grey sky while breathing in the fresh October air felt different somehow. His army career now history. Perhaps best forgotten. He had things to do. A new life lay before him. All he had to do was settle a score. It was true he told himself. As much as he wanted to simply move on it wasn't going to happen. Not while the man who put him behind bars was free and unaccountable for what he did. Fifteen years in prison is a lifetime, especially for someone who had been so active. Someone who had planned a future that would have been better than anything he had experienced due to prison. His life had been shattered by a single individual with influence and power. A nasty piece of upper class trash.

Once upon a time he had respected such people. Once upon a time he had even considered them better than him, but not anymore. He had seen these people for what they were and no longer held any illusions about their artificial superiority.

The grey sky above made spotting a drone easier without the Sun blinding him. Its presence not unexpected given the people he was dealing with. He was a threat, and they would monitor him until the threat went away. They had made him an offer to placate any anger issues he might possess over serving fifteen years behind bars for something he didn't do. Maybe if they hadn't bothered he might have simply emigrated anyway. That they did meant they knew he was innocent, and they were the government.

Something he had learnt during his trial was that government lawyers did not differentiate between right and wrong. Not those at the Ministry of Defence (MOD) anyway. They operated on a friend or foe basis. Any challenge was a foe.

They had given him twenty-four hours to decide to leave the country. Not a long time to choose to remain or emigrate. But thinking that way ignored their arrogance or how they categorized people like him. Handing him a bag full of money and one way ticket to the other side of the world where he would be out of harm's way. At least that's what they wanted him to believe. He had worked for them too long to accept they might have changed tactics dealing with any kind of threat. Chances were that he would die suddenly, a hit and run or fall from a clifftop. Threat eliminated. That's how they operated in his day, and he supposed somethings were never likely to have changed.

Getting him out of the country on his own two legs was what they needed not to attract unwanted attention. His death could happen any time after that. The responsibility of another country's law enforcement was unlikely to be headline news in the UK.

So, they were watching what he did while he was here. What did people do in the last twenty-four hours before emigrating? Who knew? Thing was while he was watched they would be comfortable that he was following their instructions. The moment he deviated or disappeared every red bulb would light up the phones at the MOD, and from then on he would be a legitimate target. It crossed his mind that they would give him a target title and wondered what it might be? Kill Priest. Nah, too obvious. Ring the Chapel Bell. Possible.

A white Mercedes sports drew up in front of him while he stood debating with himself the most likely title they would use for his assassination assignment. Inside a black female driver lowered the passenger window and leaned towards him, "Leo Priest?"

"Puss in Boots?" he replied leaning on the car eyeing her ever so tight top barely able to contain an ample cleavage that appeared genuine rather than cosmetic.

"You expecting anyone else?" A bright white smile lit up her pretty face.

"Not today" he said, opening the door and climbing in. Apart from an ample cleavage a very short skirt revealed long smooth thighs above knee high boots. The image made him recall something he had been missing for so long. It was an effort not to stare.

She held out a hand "Two hundred and fifty quid."

Business brought him back to the reality of his situation "I was told two hundred."

"You were but that was yesterday."

"Guess I should have checked the inflation rate," he said, without moving. If she were considering fleecing him then he preferred to get another ride. Which was a shame because the view was seriously good. They sat quietly for a couple of minutes before he said, "You think I have it on me?"

"I know you do" she said. "I've friends on the inside too. They told me a lot about you. An innocent bad ass."

"You said '*innocent*' like you didn't believe it?"

"If I had a penny for every con who claimed innocence I'd be spending today in the Bahamas not giving you a ride. I'm just here for the money, so either pay up or get out."

No one ever believed a con. Even cons didn't believe cons why should she be any different? He just wished someone would take a long hard look at him and see he wasn't lying. Digging into a trouser pocket he pulled out a wad of cash and thumbed off two hundred and fifty pounds. She accepted it without thanks and slipped it between her ample breasts.

"Now you can tell me where you want to go?"

"Romford, Essex. Know it?"

"I know it. Whereabouts?"

"I'll tell you when we get there. By the way there's a spy in the sky."

"You just paid an extra fifty for it. I spotted it while I was waiting for you a few hundred yards back. I always arrive early to spot uninvited guests."

"You might have told me. I'd have been less resistant to paying the extra."

"But then I wouldn't have gotten to see your reaction."

He chuckled she was turning out to be just what he'd been told to expect. Maybe better looking? "Doesn't it bother you having someone watching you at work?"

She made a face "Man, I've always got someone watching me. It comes with the territory."

Priest made himself comfortable while she focused on the road. Puss in Boots was a high-class prostitute who knew one of the inmates he had gotten friendly with. She came highly recommended by cons likely to be choosey who drove them. Also, she was up for almost anything. All he had to do was ask and meet her price. You never know when you might need a hand hunting bad guys. The silence between them felt a little tense but nothing he couldn't handle. Silence it was, he thought. After a half hour the silence proved too much for her and she broke it with a question.

"Why'd you kill that girl?"

It brought him up with a start. "What part of innocent did you misunderstand?"

"You don't have to be modest with me. You're a killer. All soldiers are killers. You've served your time so they can't charge you again."

"I wasn't trying to be modest," he grumbled. "Killing a young kid like that was murder. When a soldier kills he's doing his duty."

She glanced at him in the rear-view mirror, just long enough to catch and momentarily hold his dark eyes. "You're pretty convincing, so why didn't the court believe you?"

"Because the real murderer had professional help to make me a scapegoat."

"You mean this guy you were supposed to be bodyguarding?"

Suddenly she knew more about his case than expected. "You checked me out?"

"I wouldn't live long if I didn't check out everyone who pays me for a ride in that seat."

"I take it you don't think me all bad otherwise you wouldn't be giving me a ride?"

She shot him a quick smile, "Don't flatter yourself. I can look after myself as well as any man. Don't let these boobs and long legs make you misread what I'm capable of when pushed."

"Never entered my head," he replied.

"Yeah, sure," she grinned. "You've been looking me over since you climbed in. Forget it, you couldn't afford me."

"You mean my winning personality hasn't won you over?"

"Is that what that is, man you're going to have to brush it up more than just a little."

"What made you choose to be a hooker?"

It was her turn to be caught off guard. With eyes fixed on the road, "Haven't been asked that since I last saw my mother more than a dozen years ago. I'll tell you what I told her. I'm a non-conformist who never wanted to simply survive. D'you think I'd been driving a forty grand machine if I'd joined the system as someone's assistant?"

"You did it for the money," he said.

"Damn right I did it for the money!" She snapped, "These days I'm a thirty-year-old hooker facing imminent retirement. I saved hard and invested well thanks to a few knowledgeable clients. Next year I'll be living in a warm climate sipping margaritas on a beach."

"And you won't miss the life," he said.

"Now I know you're kidding," she laughed. "So, what about you, what are you intending to do with the rest of your life?"

"After I've resolved a few outstanding issues I'll be emigrating, possibly to Australia. Somewhere in the Pacific because I like the sound of it."

"I take it those unresolved issues have to do with your innocence?"

He turned to her. Noting slim muscular arms with protruding triceps that indicated plenty of exercise. Thighs equally muscular. "Maybe."

"Will you need help?"

"Better that I do this alone. No one else needs the kind of shit storm likely to explode. Especially, someone intending to retire to a sunny beach next year."

"I wasn't offering to do it free," she asserted. "We're talking fifty thousand if you ever need my assistance."

"You think someone like me has access to that kind of money?"

"I think someone like you always keeps a well-hidden stash. You've been in war zones, and you wouldn't be the first soldier to grab valuables you stumbled across. I read about gold bars going missing in Iraq. Your unit was operating in the area at the time."

"Wow you just made a heck of a leap. There were dozens of units operating around that region at the time. Anyone of them could be responsible."

"Most of them would have been captured had they been responsible. This needed someone with brains and connections to figure a way to get the gold out of Iraq."

"Why would I have remained in the army if I'd taken the gold?" He asked.

"A clever bloke would have carried on as normal for a few years. After the loss was forgotten he'd move on."

"I was still in the army when arrested."

"What happened to you was unexpected. You weren't on combat duty anymore. Maybe you were preparing to leave before the shit hit the fan. Then you killed that girl."

"I did not kill that girl!" He repeated irritably.

"If you did take that gold I might believe you," she said.

"I didn't," he added.

"Shame," she replied with a glance before her gaze returned to the road.

"How come you know so much about Iraqi gold?"

"I read a lot, especially about things such as stolen treasure," she said. "Wherever there's a war someone's profiteering and not only munitions manufacturers. People are opportunistic by nature. I'm proof of that. Picking up the odd gold bar as you're passing one of Saddam's banks wouldn't have been the same as robbing it."

"Sorry to disappoint," he said.

They arrived at the location in Romford an hour later. A corner red brick three bedroomed property empty for the past fifteen years.

"What's this place?" She asked as he climbed out.

"Home," he said closing the door.

"Looks like you've someone keeping the place tidy for you. I didn't think you had a partner?"

"Family took care of it. Thanks for the ride."

As she drove off he noted the static drone high overhead. Still                                                    watching.

# CHAPTER TWO

*Dad*

Knowing your father was an alcoholic didn't help the relationship. Not that it was meant to. Priest just wished his father would at least try to stop drinking, even for a few days. He'd had fifteen years in which to do it while his only son was locked up. Not that the price for his help didn't facilitate his addiction. A couple of bottles of Jack Daniels each week had purchased his unflinching conscientious support. Over seven hundred and eighty weeks and fifteen hundred and sixty bottles later. Priest had no idea how his liver had survived the test of time.

Inside he found his home almost spotlessly clean with everything as he had left it. His father had kept to their deal. Employing and monitoring cleaners and any workmen needed to maintain the property in good condition. Cheap for the price.

He dropped onto a sofa in the front room and picked a phone off its cradle. These days it would be considered an antique. His father answered as if waiting for the call.

"Son, is that you?" He asked excitedly.

"Sure is dad," he replied. Odd, he thought. No matter how much he complained about his old man his father always sounded pleased to hear his voice. "You coming over?"

"Just needed the invitation. See you in fifteen."

Living locally helped him keep an eye on his son's property with as little hassle as he could bear. After purchasing the property using his father to maintain it during his absence overseas had proven useful. It also meant that he could stay in contact. The property provided him a base, something never offered by either of his parents. Funny, but for the first time in his life it meant he belonged somewhere other than at an army base.

His father arrived on the dot and got ushered into the front room. The smell of alcohol following in his wake.

"I noticed the drone outside. D'you think they bugged this place?"

His son nodded, "Highly likely. They've given me twenty-four hours to provide an answer they want to hear."

"Are you going to give it to them?"

"I'm working on it."

"All this trouble over a guilty man who served his time," he sneered. "Doesn't make sense."

"Unless I'm innocent," he reminded him.

"Wow, so this is what it's like playing against the big boys," his father sniggered. "They truly are a bunch of bastards!"

"They want me out of the country. Australia came highly recommended."

"Gosh, that's the other side of the world we'll never get to meet."

"You can come with me if you like?"

"Nah, I like it here."

"Did you do what I asked?"

"In fifteen years have I ever let you down?" His father smiled. "I know I owe you for being the way I am. It's what pushed you into joining the military. I'm weak, but still care about you. It felt good having something to do for you, even if it was just keeping this place clean and tidy."

Priest nodded. His expression revealing nothing. "Can you remain here until I get back?"

"Sure, it's cleaner than my place. What about…."

"The bottle's in the drinks cabinet," he replied flatly. "I may be a few hours." His hand gesturing differently. They had a hand code that spoke volumes.

"Sure son, you take as long as you like. I'll be waiting."

He called a cab and got taken to a cemetery between Manor Park and Wanstead opposite a stretch of open fields known as Wanstead Flats. Telling the cabbie to wait he headed inside to a grave of an uncle. Eddie Priest. Dead twenty years. Knowing the drone remained above he knelt down and hunched forward as if in prayer. His hands digging at the earth between his knees until they reached a box handle. Clearing the earth took a few minutes. Leaving the box in place he lifted its lid. Sealed in a plastic bag a Berretta PX4 Storm with four spare clips. More than enough for what he had planned. He removed the weapon from the bag and slid it under his trouser belt. The clips went into an inside jacket pocket.

When finished he covered up the box stood up and returned to where he had the cab waiting.

Only the cab and driver were missing. Nowhere to be seen. Seconds later a Mercedes sports roared alongside. A familiar face at the wheel.

"What are you doing here?" He asked through a lowered passenger window.

Puss-in-Boots wore a wide grin, "Helping you out. The cabbie was playing for the other team."

"You know that for sure?" It was not unexpected. Drones had been known to lose targets in big cities. Bandock was *'old school'* and would want to keep close tabs on his movements. Cabbies were an easy and convenient way of doing that.

"I do," she said.

"What did you do with him?" He asked.

"Do you want a lift or not?"

"I can't pay you?"

"I'm calling this an investment," she replied.

"You still think I'm involved with Iraqi gold."

"Let's say I'm not yet convinced you're not."

"You might end up disappointed?" It was easy to recall how the military had gone to great lengths searching for the stolen treasure. Life imprisonment the penalty for those discovered in possession. Yet, somehow, the thieves had gotten clean away. Some said more than twenty million others fifty million. Few knew the truth.

"You could always call another cab?" She said snapping him back to the present.

He climbed in and the engine roared as they sped away.

This time around she was quiet concentrating on the road ahead and, he thought, perhaps wondering if she was making a mistake.

He spotted the drone out the side window. The reason for its presence more sinister. Resources would be unlimited they didn't want him getting close to any of the people, especially the man responsible for the girl's cold-blooded murder. The man responsible for wasting his life. Yet right now they remained uncertain of his intentions. Maybe prison had changed him? Slipping quietly away sensible in the circumstances. If he did they might just leave him alone, but that too was only a slim chance. He would always be a loose end, something rarely afforded. Killing him in some far corner of the world better than on home turf.

Not that he had never contemplated doing exactly that. Disappearing without a trace. The easy option, for some. But not an angry soldier. Someone trained to kill enemies to survive. Someone willing to confront hardships few would even contemplate. Being consumed by bitterness that had been allowed to fester in confinement. It was always close enough to be his reason for living. His initial rage had lasted ten years before settling down to a simmering flareup easily triggered by memories of an innocent girl's death. The last five years dulled his anger further, but now he was out something was happening that he couldn't easily explain. It was as if he had the freedom to genuinely decide what he wanted. The first time in fifteen years. Inside he felt the fire of a deep-seated rage gathering momentum. Proving the depth of hurt from a betrayal that never left demanding accountability.

Little wonder they were watching him. No doubt psychologists had been sought for their opinions about the probability of him seeking revenge. Clearly, because of the drone their opinion had leaned towards the possibility being high.

Dr Phillip Hummer who interviewed him prior to his release. Kept his questions hedging around his intentions towards his accusers after his release. Playing games with words was a skillset he had been trained in. The possibility of capture in combat scenarios always high, making training essential. The problem for Priest was that Hummer knew he was using what he had been trained in. Not that Hummer acknowledged it to him, but something like that is impossible to hide from an expert. That's why Priest was surprised that he had been given early release and unsurprised that he was being monitored.

With his insides bubbling under a fresh resurfacing rage that was proving too much for him to ignore. He allowed it to run its course just to see where it wanted to take him. Betrayal does plenty of harm and a tough emotion to recover from. People in positions of power who he had relied upon had let him badly down. There were no excuses to justify what they did. No justification that could lessen the hurt he felt. Had they done it to others? Why that even mattered he didn't know, but the thought it was not the first time raised his temperature. Where he had previously been uncertain if he would go after the real killer, anger the likes of which had never experienced squashed any doubt. It needed to be done and he needed to be the one to do it. Accountability had a place in his life, always had and he would see to it that others appreciated that.

Sometimes, Priest felt himself slow in reaching decisions. Like this one he had argued back and forth with himself over such a long period of time until quite unexpectedly his emotions took over and in this instance prevailed. He guessed it was because this had been the first time he was free to act, all other times he had been inside. However, unlike his military training this time also meant that he was following his emotions rather than logic. Ordinarily he was a man of logic. Do A to reach B. Going after the killer might not appear logical except to someone who had been shut away over fifteen years for something he didn't do. Then it made perfect sense as did seeking revenge for someone he barely knew. A young woman with her whole life ahead of her. He sighed inwardly; this was personal. His training instructors would have been upset that he wasn't following their guidance. Keep personal issues out of your head when in combat, they only blurred what you had to achieve and slowed you down.

At that moment he figured them right except for motivation. He was more motivated than he had ever been. The rage had reached his chest and wanted to explode. Over the next twenty-four hours whatever it took he would discover the identity of the killer and make him pay.

No doubt his enemies would know how deep his inner rage was better than he did. The psychiatrists would include inner rage as part of their opinion. But they could not know how powerful it was. That much at least was personal. Still, it would concern them. Maybe enough to keep a full surveillance unit on him until he caught a plane out. A full surveillance team would be difficult to lose but not impossible.

"May I borrow your phone?" He asked.

"In the glove box," she said.

He sent a coded text message waited a moment then killed the connection. Slipping the rear cover off the phone he picked out the SIM card and snapped it in two. "That'll stop them tracking us."

"Good job I didn't hand you my regular phone." She said, a small frown creasing her usually smooth forehead.

"Sorry about that, it was necessary."

"You going to tell me what's happening?"

"It's better you don't know."

"For whom?" She asked looking him straight in the eye.

"You. If they come round asking questions and you don't have anything to tell them you'll probably live through the experience."

"That's provided they believe me."

"No reason they shouldn't. My training would prevent me from discussing plans with a stranger. They hold a lot of store in what they trained me to do and how I behave.

Now I understand their reasons. It's so they can better predict my reactions."

"Are you telling me that you don't have a mind of your own?" Her question held a note of disbelief.

"Almost, except I've had fifteen years to lose some of their conditioning. That's why I've chosen to resolve a matter that greatly bothers me emotionally."

"Do you really expect them to pay me a visit?" She asked less certain she wanted the experience.

"It's not unthinkable. Just do as they ask, and you'll be fine." He glanced at her as she turned back to the road ahead. "What're you thinking?"

"That I charged you too little." She griped.

"I warned you about that."

"Yeah you did, but the fact they're watching you so closely might mean they also think you've got that gold. It'd make more sense than your innocent story."

"Give me strength!" He said. "Okay, have it your way but whatever happens to you is because you refused to listen to me." Being angry with Puss-in-Boots was a waste of energy but her knowing what the people he was dealing with were capable of meant she was putting herself at unnecessary risk. He really didn't want another dead woman associated with his name. Yet she had already taken any possibility that Bundock would ignore her out of his hands.

If nothing else the thought that she might now be in danger motivated him to follow through with something he had considered long and hard. Although, without ever really knowing if he would actually follow it through. His text message had changed any notion that he would simply slip away. The text message made a commitment to allies that they prepare.

By the same time the following day he would either have succeeded in dealing with the killer or be dead himself. Dr Hummer, the psychiatrist, had sewn a seed of anxiety by suggesting that he wasn't as sharp as he had been in his twenties. He was possibly right, but staying fit had been a priority. Regular daily exercise and practising martial arts in his tiny cell, even in the cramped confines he'd made it work for him.

Also, the long spell in prison had introduced him to a side of himself that he might never have discovered. Depression and loss of self-confidence had taken a toll and although he had survived but fallout remained a strong possibility. Especially in regards his abilities dulled by years of imprisonment and no adversaries to keep his speed honed. Also, like it or not the aging process did slow down his reaction times. That much he could feel and see for himself.

The human body hits its peak around twenty-five and sustains itself at that peak over the next five years. From thirty onwards the body goes through a gentle decline. Bones no longer repair as quickly as they once did because they stopped growing while muscular development continues. However this means that flexibility after thirty becomes hampered by stiffening. Additionally, eyes, ears, and senses are fully developed and functioning as they should. Recovery from injury remains quick even with slower bone healing. Subtle changes after thirty increase rapidly between forty-five and fifty.

The psychiatrist had done a good job on him raising concerns over his physical prowess, especially against younger equals. Yet he stubbornly refused to be so daunted as to deny himself an option that would bring accountability to a killer who deserved to die.

Another seed sewn by Hummer related to his military career and damaged reputation. A reputation in tatters meant the only thing he had left to lose was his life. Bizarrely the idea that his life should mean something more to his enemies acted as a spur to track down the killer. Those present at the high court did not include the killer. But that did not stop those there from denigrating his character with lie upon lie until even he wondered about his innocence. The case lasted a week and by the end of it he understood why the jury could do nothing other than find him guilty. Not that it made it easier to bear. He had been sentenced to twenty years and was out in fifteen for good behaviour. A small smile grew on his face as he played with how those who had lied would have reacted to news of his early release. Not well he hoped.

Recalling the night it happened was like a repeating nightmare. Those responsible had destroyed two lives. It had been late in the evening whilst he was on duty as a military bodyguard. Part of the Military/Police Co-operation Unit (MPCU) for U.K. homeland security. Wearing civilian clothes so as not to stand out he had been patrolling a corridor at a luxury London hotel in which their High Value Target (HVT) was accommodated. As a new seconded team leader, he was especially careful taking time to walk the perimeter searching for anything that others might have missed. His Head of Section, Ralph Bundock was a young career-focused nob. With an abundance of family connections throughout government and virtually untouchable should anything go wrong. Any blame would lie squarely on Priest's shoulders.

He had been checking the floors and rooms directly above and below the HVT. The rooms were meant to be vacant for the duration of their stay and he had been issued a master key card for access to both. Entering the room below he heard a commotion overhead that caused the ceiling lights to tremble. Possibly a fight. Racing out he headed up the emergency stairs.

Two of his team stood outside the door to the HVT's suite. Gorman and Harris. Smart in fitted dark suits, ties, and brilliant white shirts. Their black shoes buffed to an immaculate shine. They had to have heard the commotion but remained fixed to their post. He wasn't familiar with either until meeting them for the first time that morning after being assigned their team leader. He would have preferred to have had more time to become acquainted, but time was short.

"Are you two deaf?" He said reaching out with the key card.

They didn't move. Blocking him.

Harris said "He doesn't want to be disturbed, Sergeant."

"Step aside," he replied. Meeting the other man's gaze. They were both around six feet tall. Harris an inch taller.

Both large, fit, and ready to react. A brief unexpected hesitation. Defiance? Priest wasn't sure. A glance between the two before they obeyed. A mental note to talk to them later.

Inside. The plush suite was warm. A place of luxury, style, and comfort. Large paintings on neutral-coloured walls. Leather sofa, deep redwood furniture. A silent fifty-inch LCD TV. The glass doors to a small balcony overlooking the river open. The HVT had been instructed not to venture out. A scalloped grey chair lay on its side across a rich thick pile carpet. Beside it a spilled wine glass on top of a red stain. The dark metal Sig P229 slipped into his hand from its leather underarm holster safety off. Cautiously, he stepped towards the balcony. His men close behind.

The HVT was face to face with a small pretty brunette. Her expression fearful. Desperate. Hands trapped by her sides as the HVT moved in for a kiss. Her back pressed hard against a waist-high metal railing. Below the city lights and sounds a reflection of normality.

"You shouldn't be out here," Priest said.

The HVT glanced back suddenly angry. A frown distorting his bearded features. In his forties with rounded shoulders. His shirt pulled out of his trousers flapping in a slight breeze. A look of contempt as he caught Priest's gaze. A man accustomed to others obeying without hesitation. "Get out!"

He took in the brunette. Familiar. Someone employed as a secretary at the office. Admin support staffer. Tears ran down her cheeks. Eyes pools of terror. The front of her dress torn exposing a black bra. He holstered the Sig.

"Please, don't leave me" she pleaded.

"I told you to get out!" The HVT said. He was middle height, medium build. Holding her wrists as she struggled.

"Let her go," Priest ordered.

"Do you know who I am?" The HVT irritably asked more than a little surprised by the military man's hard tone.

"I couldn't care less. Let her go!" He repeated. Bundock had gone to great pains keeping the identity of the HVT anonymous. Sometimes that was the way it was. Code words. An alias. Priest was here as protection nothing more, although that included from himself on occasion, and this was one of those occasions.

"Boss, maybe we should just leave them?" Harris said from behind.

"Not happening," he said. "Are you seeing what I'm seeing. We walk out of here and she gets raped. She's one of ours. Her family would be rightly disappointed in us if that happened. Don't you think?"

"We're his protection team, nothing more" Harris reminded him.

"Agreed and right now we're protecting him from himself. Wouldn't do if one our client's was later arrested for rape on our watch."

"You just made a critical error that will follow you for the rest of your life," the HVT spoke dispassionately. A man of ice. "You have no idea how much trouble you're in, but you're about to find out."

He released the girl's wrists and dropped down in a squat by her feet. Grabbed her ankles and flipped her backward over the railings. No second thoughts. No hesitancy. Her scream could be heard as she plummeted to the ground a hundred feet below. Priest just had time to take a single step forward before a blow to the back of the head knocked him unconscious.

****

When he came round he was alone in a cell laid out on a bunk. It was still dark outside with the Moon visible from a barred window. He had been undressed. Left in shirt, trousers', and slip-on shoes. Raising his head off the pillow excited a stabbing pain at the back of his head. He reached a hand back and gingerly ran his fingers over a lump at the base of his skull and sighed. Sitting upright he took in the dull grey green surroundings. Police cell he concluded, the smell of vomit and waste hung in the air from previous users. So many had used the tiny confines for vomit space the stench would never leave.

An hour passed before the cell door opened. A man followed by an armed uniformed police officer stepped inside. In his mid-forties, he wore a tired tweed suit, tie, and grey shirt in contrast to a pair of smart brown shoes. "Would you like some breakfast?"

"Why am I here?" He asked.

"Forgotten already?" The man grinned without humour.

Priest frowned casting his mind back. The girl. Her desperate plea. The HVT flipping her over the railing. Her scream. Jumping to his feet he exclaimed, "The girl!"

"She's dead. Falling a hundred feet does that. Her name was Michelle Baez."

"I tried to save her. We were protecting a High-Value Target. He was attacking her."

"Your men claim you attacked her and your client," he replied. Gaze fixed. Tone neutral.

"That's insane!" He said, glancing at the uniformed officer. "I've only just joined the unit. Most of my time has been in combat Iraq        Afghanistan. This was my first home tour and as a protection team leader. I wasn't going to screw up by murdering an innocent. I told you I tried to save her."

"They said you'd make this difficult. Apparently it's something you're trained to do. But legally I'm supposed to hear your side of things even when it's bleeding obvious you're lying." He slipped his hands into trouser pockets and flexed his heels, so they lifted off the ground. "I don't know maybe you're suffering from PTSD or maybe that's what you want us to think. Your own men claimed your intended target was your client, the girl just got in the way."

"They're lying" he shook his head in disbelief.

"Why would they do that?" The policeman asked.

"To protect the client. He's someone special, probably with powerful friends. He was going to rape the girl. I couldn't let that happen."

The policeman shrugged, "You'll get your chance in court but if I were you I'd plead guilty. It's the only way you'll receive any sympathy."

"But I'm not guilty!" he said.

"Your own men corroborated that you attacked your client. That the girl was collateral damage, isn't that what you blokes call the unlucky ones?"

"It wasn't like that" he said, staring down at the floor as if searching for answers.

"Luckily your client survived" he sighed. "You're being treated as a terrorist. That means your regular rights don't exist."

# CHAPTER THREE

*Director of Establishments*

Priest closed his eyes and feigned sleep while Puss-in-Boots drove them to the next destination. His mind playing with recent events prior to his release.

His release should have meant the beginning of a new life, even for someone branded a killer. He'd never given the idea much thought until a recent visit from the Director of Establishments, Sir Ralph Bundock. A week prior to his early release. His old boss had climbed the career ladder as expected. A pompous man now in his late fifties still carrying an over inflated ego. His presence unprecedented. It raised questions in Priest's mind that allowed him to piece together events from his trial. He had never been absolutely sure about his former manager's involvement. Certainly he had done him no favours at court, but no more than anyone else, and he alone had provided a few favourable comments. Kind words had raised doubts with Priest. He wasn't interested in pursuing anyone not complicit in his imprisonment. Those doubts prompted him to believe that Bundock was being nothing other than his customary hyper-critical self.

Bundock had appeared casually friendly in a neutral kind of way. The best he could manage with anyone he considered far below his station. To a spectator it might appear that he genuinely wanted to help. Priest had often marvelled at how some of the senior rankers, mostly Eton educated, possessed a talent to feign friendship and warmth towards their staff even when the exact opposite were true. It was a skill set. Something he had never managed to acquire. What you saw is what you got he'd been told about himself more times than he cared to remember.

The question that intrigued him most was why Bundock felt it necessary to step down from his lofty haven to meet with him? Why bother after all this time? Priest was a nobody. A soldier without a country. Remaining quiet for most of the visit was easy. allowing the other man to prattle on while ignoring the deep rifts that divided them. *'Water under the bridge'*, he heard him say. Referring to fifteen years unwarranted imprisonment. The Director of Establishments should have read his file more carefully. It would have saved time. Priest had been compared to a heat seeking missile on several occasions. Overcoming all obstacles. It should not have proved much of a leap for his former boss to figure that he would not be deflected once his mind was set. Yet Bundock was too arrogant to see beyond his own capacity to be motivated by vengeance rather than someone trained to kill for less. The Director of Establishment's career was all important in his personal arena and viewing everyone around him as sharing that importance relegated the possibility of an alternative motive as slim at best. *'Don't rock the boat'*, was the next piece of advice he heard before Bundock clarified that he was fully aware of the circumstances surrounding the incident in which a young woman died.

The pompous bastard knew he was innocent, knew the entire truth. Yet had gone along with the cover-up. Perhaps it was the reason he was now Director of Establishments? His visit finally began to make sense. He had read his file and knew his reputation for hunting down targets. The prospect of Priest pursuing him when so close to retirement an unwanted blip on the length of his lifespan. *Shame.*

Priest nestled back on the seat only half listening while Bundock warned that the Establishment were watching. Making a nuisance would be dealt with quickly and no one would mourn his passing. Significantly Priest learned that the Director of Establishments had indeed played a pivotal role in the cover-up orchestrating the action that needed to be taken so the HVT remained '*clean*'. The *old boys network* at its best.

While Bundock dug his own grave Priest's dark eyes flashed with anger. Suppressing a powerful urge to attack the other man. Punching the reinforced glass that separated them would have cost his release. Perhaps that had been the reason Bundock allowed himself to explain his part in his incarceration? It was devious and the type of thing he should have expected. Remaining seated as if unmoved while hearing his former boss express an initially heavy reluctance to agree to blame him for the young woman's death. His hesitation to do so overcome by powerful people who insisted so strongly that he felt his own life at risk.

*Sure you did*, Priest thought. *They had made him the scapegoat and you went along with it. You're no better than them but it's not you I want. It's the HVT.*

Bundock continued with what was obviously rehearsed and considered by the powers that be a very reasonable offer for fifteen years of someone's life. "I've been told to offer you half a million pounds to leave the country. Never to return. I hear Australia can be nice. You'd be safe there too."

Clearly another threat, but Priest was well passed threats or money. Not that he was going to pass on an opportunity to take the cash. It alone would convince some that his price had been met. "I'll think about it," he heard himself say.

"Well don't take long there's limited time after you walk out of here." Bundock returned with a more familiar steely glare that had once meant something.

"How long do I have?" He asked more out of curiosity than interest.

"After your release, twenty-four hours." He sighed, "The alternative is that you'll have a very short time to enjoy your freedom. Personally, I'd take their offer, it's pointless going after these people. You know that's good advice."

He knew they thought it was because they were from the same mould as Bundock. Wealthy families, privileged lifestyle, and an overabundance of arrogance. They felt safe. Comfortable. Unaccountable for their actions even when people died. To them there was no right or wrong. It was all about protecting their own to maintain their bubble of existence. Soon they would discover the bubble could be popped.

"Who made this happen?" He asked, the awkward question slipping out before he could prevent it.

Momentarily catching Bundock off guard. A small wry smile parted his thin lips as he answered, "You know I can't tell you that, but why ask?" Eyes narrowing gauging Priest with renewed suspicion.

"Curiosity," he replied. "It happens after you've spent fifteen years in a place like this for no reason. You get to wonder who figured it best you do."

"I hope you're not considering anything foolish Leo," he replied soberly. "Contrary to what you might believe I never did like the idea of sending an innocent man to prison. You deserve some happiness, don't spoil what remains of your life."

"I don't intend to" he said. "But you can't blame me for being curious."

"Just don't end up like the proverbial cat," he said. Shuffling on his seat to make himself comfortable leaning forward closer to the screen separating them. His voice low as he spoke, "If you do anything they consider a threat you're a dead man. I won't be able to help you. No one will."

Maybe if Priest hadn't spent so long working for Bundock he might have been taken in by his demonstration of understanding and sympathy. He was very good at convincing people he spoke the truth and perhaps occasionally he did, but not today. There was no doubting Bundock's concern, but the reason for his concern was nothing to do with Priest's welfare, far from it. After explaining his role in the cover-up he guessed he would also be a target should Priest go rogue. "I know you don't scare easily, but this is about common sense. You've wasted fifteen years of your life in here. Why end it so soon after doing such a thing?"

"You're jumping to conclusions" he replied.

"I'm reading your expression. It's neutral. That means you're thinking about whether to take the money or die attempting to kill me and the others."

"Why did you tell me about your part in this shit if you knew it would make you a target?"

"I was instructed to do so," he replied coolly, leaning away from the screen.

"They wanted you in the firing line and you obliged them." Priest understood the rationale but not what motivated Bundock to comply.

"You know how this works," he replied dismissively. "I'm potentially collateral damage. In the event you come after me first you hand them an opportunity to take you out."

"I don't have a choice now do I. You're the one who knows the identity of the HVT. Guess it's lucky for you that I'm not about to hunt him down otherwise we could have a situation."

Bundock said nothing. Sitting for several minutes studying him before rising from the chair. "You know my contact number. If I haven't heard from you within twenty-four hours after you leave here you'll be a legitimate target."

*Legitimate*. The word played in his mind as he watched the other man leave. The only legitimate targets were Bundock, and the others. With the HVT the one who put them all in awkward street.

Bundock had every right to be concerned over Priest's release. Yet the fact he had been instructed to tell him about his part in the cover-up felt twisted. Who were '*they*' with the power to give an instruction likely to prove a death sentence and feel confident it would be followed?

# CHAPTER FOUR

*Michelle Baez*

If he were honest freedom day had proven an anti-climax. The notion that freedom would raise his spirits seriously undervalued the wasted years spent behind bars. Maybe for some it was easy to put those behind them, not him. He had had plans to do so much before his arrest and would have been a long way from here if his life had been allowed to play out as he had planned it.

Overcoming the fury that others had crushed his goals by robbing him of his freedom wasn't something he'd been able to achieve. Maybe he just wasn't mature enough? A persistent need to vent his anger never far from the surface. Now that he had made his decision ensuring those who hurt him, and the girl received the punishment they deserved was all that mattered. Revenge. So many knocked the idea as a waste of time, but living with himself required it, as if part of his DNA.

Also, it wasn't just about him. The girl who died did so because she wouldn't allow a predator to abuse her. One of the most fundamental of reasons women died. She deserved revenge even more than he. Her terrified eyes a constant reminder accompanied by pleas for help. So many times over the years he wished he had gotten close enough to prevent her death. To fend off her attacker. Her death as cold blooded as any he had ever witnessed.

Michelle Baez. He had spotted her parents in court. Their grief visible from wounded expressions. Her father full of anger. Her mother wearing a glazed lost in thought look. Likely on medication, yet determined to attend court. To witness her daughter's alleged murderer receive British justice. Priest could imagine what they were thinking whenever he caught their eyes. The man responsible for stealing their child. If he were them he'd be thinking the same or worse. At least he'd had an opportunity to speak the truth for them to hear. Going over everything that happened but none, especially the twelve men and women that comprised the jury, appeared to believe him. Their annoyed expressions full of dark misguided comprehension that had nothing to do with his innocence. He watched them as they silently listened to his men and Bundock explain how difficult it was for some soldiers to acclimatise to a civilian environment coming from repeated tours in various war zones. They had claimed that he was so highly trained the killer instinct that had been honed to perfection within him was incapable of being switched-off. He was a danger to the public and would remain so for a very long time. Nothing like throwing in a splash of fear to induce the result you want. None of the jury would ever want to bump into him on a dark night.

But worse still to come as a video screen with a blanked-out face allowed the HVT to provide his witness statement from another room. His voice soft brimming with sadness as he mentioned Michelle Baez. How she spun round to confront Priest when he unexpectedly appeared on the balcony. Challenging him while he focused on the HVT and moved aggressively towards him. More predator than protector. They didn't know one another yet Priest appeared to mistake him for someone else. An enemy. A light switch moment in which the soldier kept coming for him while Baez stuck between them. His face red with anger. Out of control. They struggled momentarily before Priest trapped her arms and deliberately pushed her over the balcony. The HVT sobbed. Except for her courage his men would not have arrived in time to prevent his own death.

Priest had listened. Hearing every lie while seeing their effect on the jury. He knew then that his case was lost. That prison beckoned. Everything he had worked towards suddenly ripped from him. Medals and commissions meaningless now.

Bizarrely Bundock had proven the only begrudging ally that day. Offering a few good words about his military career that until that evening was exemplary and full of valour. Always putting the men and women under his command first and foremost. The type of thing that might have made a difference at any other time, but nothing warranted the cold-blooded murder of an innocent young woman.

"Are you okay?" Puss-in-Boots asked.

"Have you another name?"

"You can call me anything you like Leo," she smiled mischievously eyes on the road.

"What's your real name?"

"What do you think?" She teased her tongue running over brilliant white, even teeth and luscious pink lips.

"Beatrice," he replied without hesitation.

"F off!" she said.

"What then?"

"Pussy." He glanced at her with eyes narrowed. She shrugged, "What can I say, I was an unwanted child."

"Is that it?" He asked.

She passed him a sidelong look that might have past for threatening. "You have a problem. With my name?"

He stared at her in disbelief, "Who the hell does that to their kid?"

Surprise and relief filled her face, "Most people laugh or make a joke."

"Are you kidding" he scowled. "Names are what we have to survive on for life. They're who we are. Yours made sure you didn't have it easy."

"Too right. School was a bitch, even the teachers used to tease me over it. If I hadn't been feisty I might've topped myself." She paused and gave him a long look. "Thanks for not laughing. If you had I'd have dumped you on the road."

"Some parents don't have a right to have kids. Not your fault you appeared after their five minutes of fun."

"I guess your name suits you. Leo stands for lion. It's who you are. So what was going on with you just then, nightmares?"

"I wasn't dreaming."

"Your lids were closed, and your eyes were busy, something was going on. You definitely weren't at ease."

He sighed, "I was remembering the face of the girl they say I killed."

"Haunts you does she." She said bluntly as if it was to be expected.

"You could call it that, a haunting. A bad memory." He said. "Especially when you know you should have reacted differently. I should've saved her."

"You're feeling guilty," she replied. "But from what I read you claimed you were too far to reach her in time."

There it was again she had done her homework on him. "That doesn't stop me from knowing that I should have moved sooner." he said.

"But you didn't expect your client to flip her over the railings. You couldn't have done, no one would've seen that coming." Suddenly she sounded like she was on his side as if she believed his story.

"All my training had been to make me react instinctively to situations of that kind. I failed and she died."

She shook her head in disbelief, "Bloody hell Priest you are one deep son of a bitch. You're meant to be a cold-blooded killer. The way they described you you're an assassin with ice in your veins. Yet here you are blaming yourself for not saving a girl who no one could've saved!"

"I'm not anyone."

"You're not Superman! Damn it Priest we're all fallible. Sometimes we hesitate for the wrong reason. You were there to protect a client who turned out to be a psychopath. Who knew?"

He didn't reply resting his head against the head rest and closing his eyes again.

"I guess what happened has haunted you over the past fifteen years," she said.

Was he haunted? Only for not being able to save her. No one could understand. How could they? He had a reputation for being the best of the best. Second to none. He had carried it with pride especially when it often arrived ahead of him which meant no one asked if he was up for the job. It was taken for granted no one else was better able. How the mighty had fallen. Today he was just another '*has been*', guilty of murdering an innocent.

"If you had saved her do you think they would have allowed either of you to live?"

He glanced at her dark-skinned profile. She was beautiful he thought with ebony features that defied the hardship she must have endured to reach this point in her life. It had been a long time since he had been near a woman, especially one so beautiful. The urge to touch her to feel her softness rushed through his head. He closed his eyes again, "Maybe not."

"I'm damn certain they wouldn't. Not if they'd already gone to so much trouble to make you the guilty one."

She was right. Not that it made a difference to the outcome other than he was alive and Michelle Baez was dead. However, the fact she had pointed out an alternative in a scenario with very little room to manoeuvre for Bundock and chums meant something. Maybe he had been allowed to live to avenge them both? Perhaps it was fate's twisted way of dealing with such dilemmas?

Never taking her eyes from the road she said, "You're either the most convincing liar I ever met or you're actually innocent. I'll admit you've got me wondering. What do you intend doing to them if you get the chance?"

His eyes opened again drinking in her beauty. This time she caught him studying her in the rear-view the familiarity of what she saw made her flash a knowing smile. "It's been a long time hasn't it Priest? I know the look." At least she didn't sound offended.

"Yeah, it's been an age," he grunted before adding, "If I'm so convincing why did I just spend the last fifteen years locked up?"

"I'm sure you're not the first innocent bloke to serve time," sucking in a deep breath before continuing. "This bloke, the one who killed her, do you have any idea who he is?"

"None, but I know a man who does."

"Is that where we're headed now?" She asked.

"Indirectly. I need you to drop me outside the tube station and this time go home. The next few hours are going to be decidedly risky and anyone with me will be included on a death list."

"Doesn't sound healthy, but I can play bad ass too. Shame though."

"What do you mean?"

"I mean you just served fifteen years of your life behind bars. They robbed you of those years I'd be inclined to make them suffer the same."

"They murdered Michelle Baez."

"Another reason they deserve to spend time watching their lives tick away rather than just killing them."

"You think they'll get justice in a British courtroom?"

"No," she replied flatly.

"Then what?"

"Do you know where the worst prisons on this planet are to be found?"

He frowned, "Russia?"

"Nah. Venezuela. A place called Sabaneta in Maracaibo. If you can afford it I'd have those bad guys you hate so much locked up over there for fifteen years. Not that they'd last that long, but each day will be true hell for them."

"How do you know so much about it?"

"A drugs client I know told me. He called it the grimmest place on Earth. You really need to consider it. If you need transport getting them there I can help with that too." She gauged the direction his reasoning was headed before adding, "I'd want the bastards to live in hell rather than giving them the easy way out, which is what death is."

"I'll think it over. Either way after I get things done I might need you for another ride. Can you get another vehicle, something less obvious and more robust?"

"Robust," she repeated the word slowly. "You mean something able to withstand damage."

"Yeah, that's what I mean."

Dropping him off outside Mile End station she said, "Priest, do one thing for me."

He closed the door and leaned in over the open window, "What's that?"

"Don't die."

He grinned, "You starting to care?"

"I've just invested time and fuel on you. If you had a hand in the gold heist I hope you remember me with a little gift. Not dying is the only way you can do that." Her reply kept things between them strictly business, but he wasn't convinced it was the only reason.

"If it's any consolation I don't intend dying. As for the gold," he shrugged. "You risked your time and fuel and may do it again but I might not be who you think I am where it's concerned."

"Guess I'll have to wait to find out. See you later then" she said.

"Maybe." He shrugged again, not that he was indifferent to their meeting he simply didn't know if he would be around for it to happen.

As she drove off he took the opportunity to scrutinise the pedestrian traffic round him. It would be naïve to believe

Bundock wouldn't have him followed on foot. If the Director of Establishments was worried enough to pay him a personal visit in prison, the likelihood of surveillance was a no brainer.

Catching a Central line train to a Circle line connection was the first stage of his plan. The Circle line operates as a loop which means you can start and end your journey at the same station. Walking slowly between trains making each step slower than the previous until he was overtaken by almost everyone he slowed even more to glance back at who remained behind him. Just a single guy a dozen feet behind. Their eyes never made contact, that was always best when following someone. The carriage he climbed in was half empty with vacant seats facing the double doors so that he could see who came in and out. Making himself comfortable he checked his watch. Four hours before he needed to be somewhere. Good enough. The looped journey would provide him an opportunity to spot all members of any surveillance team. The one who had remained following slowly behind had already gone. Replaced by another he had yet to identify.

There's a trick he had learned to spot surveillance operatives. Stare hard at people around you and those who look up and stare directly back will usually be innocent. Surveillance officers don't like to be spotted so they'll never glance up in your direction no matter how hard you stare.

***

The operations room of the Overwatch Surveillance Unit (OCU) monitoring Priest was sited beneath MPCU headquarters in London. A concrete structure with a single guarded entrance. The room occupied by a team of seven operators including a team leader and a state-of-the-art Artificial Intelligence (AI), to provide intuitive advice about a target's options. The walls surrounding the operators were full of large widescreen monitors with coverage of areas in London of interest.

With innumerable links to external security cameras around the United Kingdom the AI provided the kind of coverage that would have daunted George Orwell's fears of a totalitarian state. However, instead of spreading fear it was reputed to be the most advanced monitoring system in the world capable of countering terrorism by offering an educated opinion about a suspects behaviour. Reading actions, body language and lips when possible.

While human operators monitored separate screens at the back of the room and the AI managed all primary screens in front. The OSU Team Leader sat on a central platform overlooking his entire domain while able to converse with the AI. Discussions with an AI had initially been odd. It was a machine, even if it could offer knowledgeable advice. Its synthetic voice attempting inflections to mimic a human. It was always learning. A machine educating itself on how humans thought acted and spoke. After six months Jim Stacey had grown accustomed to it, even caught himself believing it was sentient. Difficult not to when so much depended on its unemotional judgement.

While conversing with the AI through a headphones microphone he was caught off-guard when interrupted by unexpected visitors. Bundock, Harris and Gorman arrived in front of him. Stacey, a mid-thirties Grade Three Crown

Servant with a fifteen-year service history found the interruption unsettling. Unexpected arrivals always made him nervous. He hated having anyone looking over his shoulder as if waiting for the moment he made a mistake. Times that by ten for the Director of Establishments. Their entrance brought Stacey out of his seat with an expression full of curiosity and nervousness.

"We've an interest in Priest. Just wanted to see if he intends to behave," Bundock said.

"Are you anticipating problems, Sir?" Stacey asked. The reason for the Director of Establishment's visit clearly above his pay grade. But this was his terrain. Here he held the power. Well that's what he would tell himself.

"You never know," Bundock replied glibly. "He was one of the best in his day, and a true rebel."

"He has a drunken father but no friends, as far as we know. Difficult to imagine that he'll not take the Australian escape route he's been offered." Stacey said.

"I want him followed until you're a hundred percent certain that he's on the Australian flight tonight."

"Is there something I should warn my people about?" Stacey asked. Concerned that he might have tasked an unarmed surveillance team to follow an antagonistic target. The documentation he had received and passed to the team read 'Routine No Threat' (RNT). However, it wouldn't be the first time something had been omitted. Bundock's arrival with two others appeared to confirm his suspicions.

"No." The Director of Establishments replied. "Let me know if he deviates from his instructions. That's all. He has six hours to reach Heathrow."

The three men left with Stacey watching after them. He didn't care for Bundock, not many his rank did. He was an overbearing narcissist with the temperament of a cold-blooded rattle snake. Completely untrustworthy and extremely dangerous because of it. Any thought of challenging him dissipated into the ether as he returned his focus to the surveillance.

# CHAPTER FIVE

*Experience Counts*

Spending four hours on the same train as it travelled round in circles was not the most boring thing Priest had ever done. Coming out of prison meant it gave him an opportunity to spot changes in the way people dressed and appeared. More people wore tattoos and metal fastenings of one sort or another especially women. He had never been one for adorning his body with metal. Perhaps because of half a dozen shrapnel burns that left his back and chest scarred in a uniquely grotesque way. However, a tattoo on his right bicep revealed he had served with 'The Rifles.'

He had also picked up on a large number of people complaining about government failures. Nothing new there. Most notably was that few in the growing numbers that climbed aboard after leaving work showed any sign of happiness. It wasn't just the job they were unhappy about, there seemed to be a kind of malaise over what was happening with the country. It was odd and, something he hadn't anticipated. It certainly made the notion of emigrating to Australia sound good.

Rising from the seat he stepped out onto a platform at Euston Square. The team came with him. Front and rear. Euston station was designed to facilitate access to both over-and underground train services. That aside, it was equipped with more security cameras than found at the

Olympic games. The surveillance team felt comfortable while he remained within its huge glass walls on the ground floor. Easily losing themselves among regular commuters while Priest moved slowly through the large complex.

Outside was a different matter. Particularly after he climbed aboard a pedal cycle and rode off into traffic. From that moment he knew he would be considered a threat. Above him the drone pursued. Traffic congestion was on his side, and he made good progress cycling between vehicles on kerbs and along alley ways to his next transport change point. The drone remained above as if fixed by an invisible cord. He slowed, finally stopping, leaning the cycle against a wall before strolling off.

He did not stop moving as a second drone appeared. Larger, heavier than the first moving at speed towards the other before ramming it so hard the surveillance drone tumbled from the sky. A dark plume of smoke in its wake. The moment it hit the road a small explosion echoed loud enough to attract attention.


A parked white van had been prepared. Anonymous in traffic among dozens of other white vans. Climbing behind the wheel the keys found hidden behind a visor together with an address and map. Priest started the engine. On the passenger seat sat a Donald Trump face mask that he pulled on before moving into traffic. Driving slowly north the visor kept his face in shadow. Not that anyone appeared to notice his obvious disguise. The side windows hadn't been cleaned in a while. None to worry about in the rear. He was on his way.

The AI at the OCU reacted immediately after the drone attack. Its synthetic male voice neutral yet commanding, "Drone down. New aggressor accomplice suggested. Examining rooftops in square mile area of attack for accomplice. Target last seen on a pedal cycle travelling North."

Stacey snatched up a phone and dialled Bundock's number. "He's deviated and has an accomplice."

"Damn! Initiate the Asset. Take him out." The Asset was an assassin. On standby 24/7. "Who helped him, do we know?"

"We're searching, but unidentified. What about the surveillance team?"

"Proceed at a distance. Caution necessary, they must not lose him!"

"This was meant to be RNT," Stacey reminded him. "Destroying a drone is not routine and initiating an Asset isn't either. I need to know what's going on?"

"Classified. Just do your job!" Bundock slammed down the phone. He didn't like subordinates demanding answers and made a mental note for Stacey to be officially reprimanded.

***

A safe house in Southgate was close to a Masonic Centre. A detached Georgian property within its own grounds. Well maintained inside and out. Priest parked the van at the back beneath a carport and headed inside. An unlocked door led into a large open plan kitchen. Its walls painted white and lined with units covered by light wooden facias. Former corporal Peter Jacks stood alongside an island divider two steaming mugs of coffee in front of him. They shook hands before Priest used a stool by the nearest mug.

Jacks was ten years older than his friend. Shorter, wider but still nimble. A short trimmed white beard making up for a balding scalp. The spectacles were new. Jacks a communications wizard and responsible for destroying the surveillance drone.

"You look better than expected Sarge," Jacks said using rank rather than a name. It was a lie, but he couldn't let Priest know what he was really thinking.

"Wish I could say the same but you're as ugly as ever corporal."

"It's a good job I don't offend easy," he snapped back with a laugh.

"How're the others?" His section in Afghanistan had comprised fourteen battle hardened individuals. Loyalty among them a 'given'. Earned from regularly saving each other. But it was Priest who had honed their survival skills and carried them through with nothing other than perseverance, compassion and wealth of experience. Combined they built the trust in Priest few others could match. By the end of the war only eight remained from their original unit. He often took comfort in the fact that had he asked they would have broken him out of prison. Squirreled him away to the other side of the world leaving the authorities without any hope of finding him. Now they were back. Older but no less formidable.

"Ready, willing and, waiting." Jacks said. "I've the building plans of Bundocks accommodation," he indicated to the plans laid out on a table. You must have made him nervous because he increased security with three teams of two back front and roof." At the table Jacks pointed out the location of each team. "They're not the regular people we'd expect."

"What does that mean?"

"Private contractors from the States. Max Protection people."

"I've heard of them even while locked up for fifteen years."

"They're the best," Jacks said.

"Why isn't he using our own people, he's entitled. Who's paying?"

"Unknown. Those guys are usually mercs from special forces. They're all armed with semi-automatics so when the show starts it's going to get loud really quickly."

"Max Protection," Priest said aloud as if envisaging the kind of people it was meant to employed. Young hardened men which could put him at a disadvantage one on one. He had been good but fifteen years locked behind bars restricted his personal training. Knowing he wasn't as quick as he had once been bothered him more than he would like to admit. Age catches up with everyone but in this arena he could die because of it.

"They'd have been tough fifteen years ago." Jacks threw in the remark hoping it might trigger a cautionary response.

"Doesn't matter who they are I'm going to take Bundock from them." Priest said adamant over his decision. He guessed what Jacks was thinking and ordinarily it would have been prudent to accept help rather than go it alone. But he was a man with something to prove to himself not anyone else. Back in the day he had been considered the best of the best. How long did a title like that last. Who knew? He didn't doubt he would soon find out though. However, he told himself relying on experience to provide what age had taken from him did not make him handicapped, just different to what he had been accustomed.

"I'm thinking Bundock isn't using his own people in case you get a chance to speak to them." Jacks said.

"Why, you think any would listen before killing me?"

"They might," he said. "A guilty bloke wouldn't still be claiming to be innocent and certainly wouldn't be pursing Bundock. Whereas the mercs from Max Protection don't give a damn what you say or the reason you're there." He said allowing Priest time to absorb his words before adding, "Bundock isn't popular. Someone as unpopular might find themselves knee deep in cack if even a suggestion of your motives were made public. There's a chance they might even reopen the case." Jacks sighed loudly, "You've got him rattled which must mean something."

"What kind of building is he living in?" Priest asked moving on.

"An empty apartment building with three levels. There's a fire escape on the roof at the back down to the ground.

It's reachable from the adjacent building's roof with an eight-foot gap between them.

"What about roof guards and cameras?"

"I'll take out the two guarding the roof and kill the cameras which are located at each corner. I'll be sited on the roof of the building across the street, it's two levels higher providing good coverage. When I'm done I leave unless you want company?"

"No, but thanks." He guessed Jacks had been thinking the same as him. Fifteen years was a long time to be mothballed and just maybe now he was passed his prime.

He turned his gaze to the floor wondering what was going on inside his own head. Was it simply an ego thing? The years he had lost were likely the best years of his life, but did he want them back so bad he was willing to die proving he still had the edge?

"You okay?" Jacks asked.

"I wouldn't go that far," he chuckled. "But you know I have to do this, don't you?"

"I know you think you have to do this, which is something different to what I'm thinking."

"Why are you helping me?"

The Corporal stared back at him with a steely gaze that might have melted ice. "You have to ask?"

It was Preist's turn to sigh out loud, "Sorry, Jacks. Guess I'm more uptight than I realised."

"We could leave now and they'd never find you," he suggested.

"And for the rest of my life I'd know the real killer of Michelle Baez was still out there enjoying his life."

"Good answer," he replied. "It means this is not all about your ego. You had me worried for a moment."

He smiled, "That's okay I was asking myself the same question."

"Just don't take unnecessary risks that you might have done fifteen years ago. You're slower, but you've plenty of skills planted in your muscle memories. If Bundock has explained the situation to these Max Power people, which I'm sure he has, they'll likely underestimate you. No one is going to expect a long-term prison inmate to be as useful as he was all those years ago."

"You blowing smoke up my arse?" He frowned, but without irritation.

"Never, but I do remember how good you were and if you think that has completed deserted you then you need to think again. Like riding a bike something stay with you for life."

Priest thought it over, prison had not offered someone like him much scope to train. Limited exercising and martial arts practice helped some, but even muscle memory required regular updates and a wider space for movement. Going up against half a dozen younger bodyguards would prove a challenge, even if Jacks took out the two on the roof. Once upon a time he wouldn't even have wasted a moment's thought on the challenge. Wow, he thought, how times had changed.

"Building security amounts to a pair of armed guards at the front reception. So, you're facing eight in all."

The Max Power mercs would be good and intent on proving themselves same as him. Two opposites eager to prove their prowess for different reasons. He couldn't afford to fail but not for himself he realised, for Michelle Baez. Civilians often mistakenly believe military personnel care little for life when in truth it is the most precious element in all theatres. The military appreciate more than most how essential the lives of their comrades are to any endeavour they take onboard. Not just in combat but camaraderie is an essential ingredient for an army to be whole. Without it no matter how well equipped they will inevitably fall apart. Lives matter most. People need people to support them in every way whether it be emotionally, mentally, or physical, they need to know someone is there for them. The family circle may be artificial, but it is no less real. That's why when a soldier kills an enemy he understands how taking a life hurts beyond his victim.

Priest had not wanted to involve his former section for fear of losing one or all, but they refused to be ignored and reminded him they were his family. With them behind him he remained a serious threat that Bundock couldn't easily remove and, after tonight the world would know they were to be included in anything involving him. The fact that he and the HVT had no idea they were in contact or indeed even in the UK a bonus. However, walking round with a death wish was never a good attitude even if it meant that he was willing to take risks best avoided. He still needed a strategy to make it work for him. Afterwards, if successful maybe he could find a place for himself in an unplanned future. That he had avenged Baez's death meant much, as it should. He had intended letting her family know the truth. While hoping to have finally brought her spirit peace. In the end he chose to leave her family alone because it would likely resurrect their grief. Instead he hung onto the slim hope that eventually the truth would reveal itself after he was finished.

Sucking in a deep breath he looked round. So much had changed. When stepping out of prison for the first time he fooled himself that he was the same man they locked up all those years ago. In reality in a world dominated by physical prowess inevitably flaws revealed themselves. Muscles less keen to react the mind beginning to miss things that a younger version wouldn't. All important for him if it meant being alive tomorrow. Bundock would never imagine him daring to breach his well-protected home the most obvious strategy would have been while he was travelling. At home in his empty apartment building he had a small army to defend against one individual. The odds in Bundock's favour would not have been missed. Priest would be considered an old man well passed his prime. Not a serious threat against the Max team he had protecting him. The notion suddenly made him feel old at forty-five.

In the event of his death only his section would grieve and maybe, his father. His loss irrelevant in the greater scheme of things. He was a nonentity. Unimportant except to those he sought revenge. While alive and in the country he remained a threat. Of course even if he took their offer he would still remain a threat, a loose end. People who deliberately and meticulously wronged others were always fearful that a reprisal would eventually catch up with them. In his line of work even more so.

He hoped Michelle Baez was looking down. If she was he felt sure she would understand and be supportive. Perhaps even want him to mete out retribution on her behalf. It was long overdue. But even if it was only his imagination playing games he figured she would agree that fifteen years behind bars gave him the right.

"Hard to believe it's been so long," Jacks said, interrupting his thoughts.

"Time flies when you're enjoying yourself," he flatly replied, an image of his cell flashing through his mind. An eight by ten with painted green walls bunk, basin and toilet. They had kept him alone. No shares. No one to discuss his case. No one to seek help from when they got out. It almost worked, but exercise in the yard and meals in a canteen gave him an opportunity to meet other inmates. Soon after, he was networking, finding out the '*screws*' who would turn a blind eye and those who wouldn't. Gradually things became easier. He had time to waste as he gradually built-up links to criminal gangs on the outside willing to contact his people. Using his father would have been too obvious and besides he didn't want to make him another victim.

"I'm going to take a shower" he said.

"I bought you some new clothes, they're on the bed. The rest of the things you need are in the shower room." Jacks watched him head upstairs. They had shared so much together it was tough seeing him as an ex-con. Priest would never admit it, but he had changed and not for the better. The old confident smile no longer present. A new haunting in his eyes revealed an unfamiliar inner turmoil. Doing what he was about to do required ice cold nerve not the flip flop burden of uncertainty. He needed to think. To consider what was for the best. Dropping onto a sofa he listened as the shower began deluging its user.

The shower took twenty minutes before Priest stepped out and studied himself in the mirror. Seeing what Jacks had seen and wishing it wasn't there. But no amount of wishing would help. He needed to go in hard without considering the possibilities. It wasn't death that frightened him it was losing. Knowing that Bundock and the HVT might never pay for their crime.

Alongside the basin a tube of black hair dye offered a quick way of brushing out the grey to make him appear younger. Pity about the rest of him. When finished he leaned over the basin hands either side and studied his own dark eyes. The new hair colour hadn't changed what he saw in them. Sucking in a deep breath he began to dress. Dark slacks, jumper socks and even a new pair of shoes that felt snug. From a distance no one would be able to tell what he was thinking. By the time he was close enough he hoped they would be dead.

"That's an improvement" Jacks said as he returned to the room.

"What's the optimum time for me to go in?"

"Ten p.m. Bundock usually reads in bed from then until eleven when he switches off the light." Jacks momentarily paused before rising and returning to the table with the apartment's layout. "He deployed one guard in the corridor outside his apartment and one on the inside. It'll take the others two and a half minutes to reach you once the noise starts," he paused again, "Are you certain you want to make this noisy as hell?"

"Positive," he said. "The noisier the better. I want the HVT to learn that I threw caution to the wind and went in guns blazing. It's not what they'll expect."

"Well we agree on that score. Though I'm not convinced it'll help us get Bundock without you being killed in the process."

"Have faith corporal," he said. "We get Bundock out of his cave with so much noise he'll know I couldn't give a damn which means his life is mine."

"Don't forget he's the man who was willing to admit he was part of a conspiracy against you because the HVT told him to do it." Jacks reminded him. "He put his own neck on the line for that bastard I'm not sure you'll be able to scare him enough to hand over his identity even using his mother."

"He dotes on her. She's the one person he cares about more than himself." Priest said.

"And what if it isn't enough?"

"Plan B." Extra dangerous than initially intended but more outrageous and defiant. Likely to trigger an immediate reaction with a high probability that Bundock would personally inform the HVT. Snatching their communication link from the ether was key to locating and identifying who he was.

Bundock would view him as reckless. Out for blood. Something easy with which to relate. Against it were the additional security precautions that would be introduced to crush him.

"You prefer Plan B don't you Corporal?"

Jacks smiled mischievously, "We all came here for a reason. To help you. Make use of us. Plan B does that. There's absolutely no reason for you to do this alone other than your ego."

He bit back an angry retort. Jacks and the others didn't deserve harsh words, especially when partly correct. "Okay, let's turn London into a war zone."

# CHAPTER SIX

*Have a Contingency*

Plan B began immediately Bundock answered his phone. Priest on the other end of the connection. "I reject your offer."

"I can't claim to be entirely surprised but hoped your prison time might have mellowed you."

"I'm as mellow as I'm ever going to get I'm coming for you. You're not safe anywhere."

"You do realise what you're doing to yourself Leo?" Priest did not reply. "You're dead the moment this call ends."

"I'll give you one chance," he replied. "Then I'll be at your door. Tell me who the HVT is and where I can find him? I don't care about anyone else involved including you. Just give me the HVT."

"I always admired your record for persistence Leo, but not this stupidity. You won't get anywhere near me no matter where I am, and in a matter of hours your face will be broadcast across the country as a sick fuck seeking revenge against the people who caught him for murder. How long do you think you can last after that happens?"

"Long enough to reach you" he said.

"You know we're already tracing this call. These days all I have to do is press a button. A team will be outside your door in minutes. You're already history."

"Bye," he said. Bundock spot on about a security team arriving within minutes. Max Protection people. Obvious by the armoured tunics and leggings they wore. It was nine thirty in the evening as he watched two black vans rush into the alley between the two buildings and half a dozen spill out of each. Unsurprisingly they headed into the building he was standing.

The buildings were eight feet apart, the fire escape ladder six. Jumping the distance easily accomplished. Jacks had already put the roof guards down from the building across the street. Three others from their section with him two brandishing grenade launchers another with a Dragunov Russian sniper rifle. Less likely to be identified as a weapon they would use.

"I'm on the roof," he spoke into a throat mic while cautiously looking around. "Hit the other building's roof access now before they reach it." Keeping casualties to a minimum necessary for the inevitable post-mortem to follow in the media.

"Bundock's at the front of the building on the third floor," Jack's voice spoke softly. "He's using a mobile to call someone."

"Get the number," Priest told him needlessly.

He was already reading the number on a laptop while a flickering red light waited to reveal its location. The call ended abruptly no answer from the other end. No location.

"Did you get it?" Priest asked.

"He didn't pick up" Jacks told him.

"Grenade launchers now!" he ordered.

Jacks checked the street for pedestrian traffic. Innocent casualties unacceptable. When satisfied he gave an all clear. A moment later the apartment building's street door erupted in a thunderclap of smoke flame bricks and wood. Tossed at high-speed cutting the air so quickly its wake was felt seconds behind. A passer-by would have been cut in half.

Priest felt the building rock beneath him as a second explosion took out the roof access on the building he had used.

"Get in there now!" Jacks shouted into the mic. "We're moving out."

As Priest rushed in through an access door bouncing a shoulder off a wall before following concrete steps down to the next level. A window of ten minutes counted down in his head.

Outside four others from his section blocked off all main roads to the apartment building. Steering heavily loaded trucks across roads and pavements. Abandoning them with smoke cannisters emptying a dense foggy mist increasing confusion as traffic slowed and stopped quickly building up as a roadblock. Two rushed to join Jacks while the others, the section's smallest headed to the apartment building Priest was finding his way around.

Encountering a fire door on the third level he dropped to his haunches leaning back against a wall stretching out a leg to nudge the door with a toe. Unbolted it gently opened barely moving before a roar of heavy lead tore through its thin wooden carcass where his torso might

73

have been. Gouging out chunks of concrete in the wall beyond. The explosion of heavy shells dumbed down his hearing. A novice would have been fazed but military experience took hold prompting him to take a quick peek through the hole in the door. Long enough to spot a bodyguard and quick enough to avoid a second round that ripped more chunks of wooden debris from the now wrecked fire door.

The second blast less intimidating as memories of combat re-filled his head. Sounds, smells and even taste. Priest closed his eyes as wooden splinter spray flew into him. His right hand automatically snatching a grenade off his belt. Opening his left eye before freeing the pin and lobbing it through the hole. Three seconds later an explosion merged with a scream before both abruptly ended.

Briefly glancing at the peppered wall. He quickly analysed the type of shot being used. Wadcutters, he thought. Unjacketed bullets with a flat front and side entirely enveloped by casing. Slower than more conventional bullets they were used in training or close combat situations for their ability to make a serious mess of a target. Something akin to a sawn-off shotgun. A big mess that could prove fatal even though it might not penetrate to a vital organ. An injury from one was intended to increase fear in an enemy. But with a short range, under fifty yards for accuracy, its abilities were limited.

A face down bodyguard still gripping the short-range weapon in a dead hand lay across the floor as he emerged from the stairs. Dust and shredded walls greeting him.

Moving slowly through the dust listening for the slightest sound of movement allowed a minute to tick by before he reached Bundock's apartment. Its door closed and no doubt an armed guard on the other side. The urgency for speed never lost on him. Whatever he had expected from himself, so far he felt satisfied.

Dropping on a knee just short of the apartment door the wall his shield. The SA80 vibrated as he blasted the door handle, ripping it off its fittings flinging it into the air. The force of the blast pushed the door inwards. Just enough for a gap to reveal a lush green fully carpeted lounge together with pieces of furniture. Part of a large sofa just visible.

The boom of another round from the wadcutter took the door clean off its hinges with wood splinters showering the corridor. Priest closed his eyes as he reared back from the blast and gave out a yell as a splinter jammed into his cheek. His right hand quickly eased the blood stained wood from his face and cast it aside without another thought, but he had already taken too long. The sound of movement inside the room just loud enough for him to catch.

Firefights more often than not go the way of the attacker due to surprise. He had been surprised distracted by peering inside the apartment too long. Meeting death head-on triggered a flash of anger. Michelle Baez would not have her vengeance, and neither would he. He had failed. More sounds caught his attention this time from the other end of the corridor. He was in trouble if he didn't move. Dropping on his belly was all he had left as the guard inside the apartment appeared, his gaze too high to see Priest early enough to aim down and fire his weapon. Priest killed him quickly as two more in the corridor raced towards him, their wild gunfire tearing into the floor either side of him. Unable to move quickly to raise his weapon he tensed expectantly on both elbows for death. Instead the pair of guards fell forward hitting the floor hard with resounding thuds as gunfire ripped the air apart directly behind them. His body relaxed on as he scrambled to his feet surprised by the timely intervention

"You alright, Sarge?" Shimmer asked, her soft voice in stark contrast after the unrelenting chatter of her weapon. No one else was meant to be in the apartment block with him. That had not been part of the plan, not part of his plan, but clearly Jacks had other ideas. He wasn't sure how he felt about it but that could wait until later.

"I owe you one," he replied standing facing the two women who came to a stop the other side of the apartment entrance. The gap enough for a guard inside to catch them in the open had they not done so.

"We're nowhere near even," Travis smiled. Her slim figure lost somewhere in baggy military garb. "We're here to make sure you make your roof delivery."

"Jacks" he said.

She shrugged, "You know what he's like. If he'd been female you could call him, mother."

"One more guard inside with Bundock," he said checking his wristwatch. "Under five minutes."

"Piece of cake," Shimmer replied stamping her feet as if running a blast of heavy lead suddenly erupted through the opening. A warning of the welcome to expect for anyone daring to enter. Grinning she met his gaze, "Just like old times. He's on the left. My shot."

Priest nodded. Shimmer threw herself low across the doorway firing left with a volley of shots that caught the guard who fell backwards into a curtained window. Entangled in drapes he dropped out of sight behind the sofa dragging the curtain with him.

Bundock stood at the other end of the room an elbow leaning against a tall white marble mantle with an open fire ablaze beneath it. "I underestimated you," he said eyeing the weapons pointed in his direction. "Are you going to kill me?"

"Not that you don't deserve it," Priest returned. "But no, I've other plans for you. We've an appointment to keep on the roof," he said with no time to waste.

"And if I don't go with you?"

A bullet tore through his right bicep with a gush of blood splattered the mantle. Bundock snatched a hand over the wound with a horrified yelp. "You shot me!"

Travis stood by the entrance weapon hot. "I'll keep shooting until you do as you're told!" The wicked glint in her eyes would convince the Devil he was in trouble.

Travis moved passed the sofa to collect Bundock without spotting the guard who had untangled himself from the curtain. leaping up from the floor a knife in his hand he caught the smaller woman from the side and pressed a knife to her neck.

"Easy," the guard said, staring at Priest. "If you value her at all you know I've nothing to lose and that I'll take her with me."

Travis didn't flinch. Her expression neutral as she stared back at Priest.

Bundock came away from the fireplace to move between them. Guessing they would not shoot to kill because he was needed. "Well it appears that you lose again Sergeant. Always being on the losing side must get you down." He took a single step forward when Priest stopped him.

"Take another step and I'll put a bullet in the back of your head. The information you've got I can find elsewhere." The steely edge to his tone was as effective as intended.

Bundock stopped just in front of Shimmer, "You're willing to lose her," he glanced back at Travis, I don't think so."

Bundock was known for bravery but he was a gambler and someone who knew the men and women who had served under him. He was correct about Priest but not Travis.

The small former soldier elbowed her assailant in the gut and twisted out of his grip, but not before his blade caught the side of her neck enough to make blood flow.

Priest threw his weapon aside and leapt at the guard to avoid shooting Travis. Bundock headed towards the door but Shimmer blocked him. Throwing a punch at her and missing was the only opportunity she gave him. Her heel came down hard on the side of his knee and he staggered before the butt of her weapon made hard contact with the side of his head.

Meanwhile Priest and the guard were trading blows. The guard not much more than half the other man's age. He was fast too, possibly as fast as Priest had once been. A jab to Priest's chin glanced off without causing damage, but gave the guard time to snatch the blade he'd dropped on the floor. Priest lifted his own blade from the sheath around his waist and the two men momentarily faced one another. Moment of truth Priest thought. Either he was going to kill or be killed. All he could do was his best.

Slashing the air the two figures came at each like gladiators. The glint of hardened steel caught the reflection of ceiling lights as they weaved and bobbed . The guard was slightly taller which provided him a longer reach. As he feinted right Priest took the bait and moved left, but the guard grinned as he stabbed his blade into the former Sergeant's arm just below the bicep. The pain was intense but quickly set aside as Priest was already moving to counter, taking the guard by surprise as he withdraw the blade, now wet with blood. Throwing his own blade from right to left hand was a trick he had learned in Afghanistan and suddenly he was glad it still worked as he drove into the stomach of the other man who appeared horrified that he had been outsmarted before dropping onto the carpet.

Helping Travis to the roof took a minute and a half. Standing waiting in a huddle searching the night for signs of their escape Priest looked toward the dark sky knowing Shimmer was watching his back and Bundock.

Travis held a cloth firmly against her neck wound. Fortunately, the blade had not penetrated deeply enough to sever an artery but it had been close.

The Director of Establishments sneered, "A helicopter will be tracked no matter how low it flies. You might as well hand yourselves in now. "

Moments later the arrival of two military stealth cargo drones trailing roped cradles appeared, their red lights flashing as they lowered directly over them. Each was equipped with four individual rotors quietly skimming the air as they stationed themselves overhead gently the cradles reached them. Bundock's sneer had quickly been replaced with something less confident.

Holding his wounded arm with his other hand the Director of Establishments hesitated at the front of the nearest cradle. "I'm not getting on that!"

Shimmer hit him just under the chin knocking his head sharply back fleetingly cutting off the blood supply to his brain. Unconscious he dropped backwards into the cradle with Shimmer climbing over him.

"See you soon," she said as the drone lifted them away.

Priest and Travis climbed aboard the second cradle and quickly disappeared into the night. Skimming low over roof tops to avoid radar but high enough not to attract attention from the ground. The city lights below revealed streets, traffic, buildings and few pedestrians. The sound of city life barely reaching them over the cool breeze that accompanied their journey.

"Well this was unexpected Travis. I thought you'd be a mum with half a dozen rug rats by now." He said, loud enough for her to hear.

She grinned, her pretty features even with a broken nose caught in the glow from a tower block. "I've a couple of kids since coming out, but couldn't resist the opportunity of finding out whether I still had what it takes. Apparently I do.

"Thank god for that," he replied.

The River Thames snakes through London on a winding two hundred- and fifteen-mile journey to the North Sea. Separating North and South London with twenty-four bridges spanning it between Kew and Tower Bridge. At night it resembles a black snake lying in a multi-coloured fanfare of lights that is the big city.

As the drones dropped lower over the river their reflection grew visible on the ceaseless lapping of small waves. A slow-moving river barge flat roofed and fifty feet in length suddenly appeared below. A dull flashing red light on its bow catching their attention as the drones headed towards it. Within minutes both drones had lowered their human cargoes onto its flat roof. Bundock barely conscious was manhandled down metal stairs into a dark hold and unceremoniously dumped on a chair under the bright glow of a single white bulb. Standing in front of him Priest and Jacks waited for him to return to full consciousness.

Studying them he said, "You really don't get it do you. I won't give you anything. I can't."

"Why?" Priest asked.

"They'll kill someone I care about. I'd sooner die."

"You mean this person," he said as Shimmer appeared beside him with an elderly white-haired woman.

"What's going on Ralph who are these people why am I here?" The elderly woman asked.

"If you hurt her I'll……"

"Who is the HVT?" Priest asked.

"What's an HVT?" The elderly woman frowned as she attempted to understand what was happening with her son.

Priest turned to her, "A man who murdered a young woman and blamed me for her murder was protected by your son. The killer is still free and I want to change that injustice."

She frowned, "That's not possible Ralph is a good boy. He enforces the law to protect us all. He wouldn't do such a thing, tell him Ralph." Bundock sat quietly. Expression revealing little other than fear for his mother. "Ralph, please tell him he's wrong."

"Lord George Cavendish," he replied loud enough for all to hear.

His mother confused with disbelief, "What have you done Ralph? George is a friend."

"You can go home now Mrs Bundock," Priest told her.

"What about my son?"

"He'll be with us for a little longer, but we won't hurt him as long as he keeps cooperating."

# CHAPTER SEVEN

*Lord George Cavendish*

Laundering money is worth billions to criminals invested in drugs trafficking and terrorism. Each year it is estimated they turn over around £90 billion in the UK and for that reason, finding people in the financial sector to help them isn't difficult.

Their job is to change the origins of the original funds. They might move the money overseas, invest it in various financial products or companies, or deposit it in an offshore account. They may also use fake ids and companies to make the process appear legitimate. Most financiers lured by the temptation of quick easy profits have established themselves over several years and thereby don't draw attention while assisting their criminal associates.

Lord George Cavendish was in his mid-thirties when first approached. Initially, he had been reluctant, sceptical, and more than a little fearful. Prison not something he had ever entertained as part of losing an occupation he thrived in. The approach by the criminal organisation had been subtle, friendly not wishing to rouse concern. The people involved, colleagues with long histories in the business. Their presence offering a modicum of assurance that all would be well. As the youngest among his peers, he was the only one to gradually surpass them in wealth. Simply by allowing himself to be drawn into criminality more deeply than any other. Being shielded from investigations as one after another either stopped or disappeared. It was a rare kind of power he had been presented with, and was quick to take advantage of it. Living in his lavish home with all the amenities he could ever desire, driving expensive cars and wearing expensive clothes, with his face plastered on TV screens as one of the UK's most prominent moneymen. Expensive cosmetic surgery had changed his appearance to a point that even relations barely recognised him. Of course, he had made himself handsome, even desirable to a few not interested in his money. The years had been good and for sound reasons he felt untouchable. Unburdened by laws or authority. The removal of fear of any accountability allowed him to do whatever he wanted whenever he wanted. Today he saw himself almost a God among men. Part of taking advantage of his unique position included deciding who lived or died to serve his personal selfishness and greed. Killing those who investigated him had been offered by the criminal organisation as a means by which he could experience the feelings and sensations of taking another's life. The power derived from it unsurpassed. Something he admitted as intriguing for it was the ultimate power any of us might hold over another.

The first time he had been clumsy. A handgun handed to him while the victim on his knees pleaded for his life. A male police officer employed by the Serious Fraud Office leading a money laundering investigation that he was involved. All he had to do was point the weapon and pull its trigger. His instruction had been to fire a single head shot. A clean kill. He stood no more than six feet from his victim's terrified face, tears running down his cheeks. His voice broken as he pleaded for his life imploring him not to do it. Cavendish held the weapon with one hand and did not hesitate, but the heavy weapon had a kick that jarred his aim, so the shell removed the man's right cheek in a crimson explosion that threw him backwards with an agonizing scream. Still alive. Cavendish finished the job with a second shot through the temple by holding the weapon with both hands. The quiet that followed eerie after the indecipherable pleas before his victim fell silent.

Standing over the body admiring his bloody handiwork. He wondered about the human being no longer of this world. Just moments ago a living breathing human with a future and, all the hopes and fears that might include. Gone now. Forever. Gone because he had cut the cord of life. Uncertain how he initially felt other than it had been necessary to protect himself. His justification, but it ignored the power buzz it also provided him. Something that lasted for several days after the killing.

Only those with him at the time recognized the signs. Killers themselves they knew one of their own. Recognized the familiar look of exhilaration evident in the eyes of an awakening psychopath. Since then he had killed a dozen more. Taking his time over each revelling in their pleas while knowing the futility of them. Sometimes giving hope before bringing it abruptly to an end. The only time it had occurred too quickly for him to adequately enjoy was the death of Michelle Baez. Flipping her off the rooftop had been too quick. Too detached. He had had no time to watch her terrified expression confront death. At the time he had played with the notion of killing Priest with a single bullet to the head, but was swayed by the bodyguards to instead use him as a scapegoat. Reluctantly he agreed. It was not missed by him that had he killed Priest at the time Bundock would not have an issue with him today.

A week shy of his sixty sixth birthday he had just received a £10 million property on the island of Jersey for his assistance in another criminal venture. Something that raised his spirits after a disappointing conversation with Ralph Bundock. It seemed surreal that the Director of Establishments would be concerned about a released prisoner impacting on their lives when the resources available to them were so abundant and their status so high.

Even now Cavendish wanted Priest killed. A simple hit and run sufficient and easily explained without a driver ever being identified. Bundock had resisted his suggestion fearing it might raise suspicions about his innocence which he had never stopped claiming. Cavendish thought his argument not enough to allow Priest to live, but gave way again against his better judgement. It was the world in which Bundock operated and therefore his expertise worth following, or so he thought. Their last conversation related to the surveillance team losing Priest. Not that he was concerned for himself or that Bundock would ever reveal his identity. The Director knew all too well the likely repercussions if he ever did such a thing. Their criminal masters would not accept the loss of someone as useful as Cavendish to their business. No, that was unthinkable, it was simply that he detested loose ends. They were so unnecessary when appropriate action could be taken to prevent them as was the case with Priest.

He sighed to himself as he climbed out of the rear of the Bentley. James Murdoch his driver holding the door open for him. "I won't need you further tonight James."

"Yes sir" the tall stocky driver replied. "Good night."

Cavendish ascended the white stone steps to his front door which opened at his approach. His butler Jonathon Veers opening it wide for him. Before closing it behind him. Veers helped remove his overcoat. "I'll be in my study for a few hours Jonathon. I heard news about an attack against Bundock and need to know what's being done."

"Yes sir, shall I bring you a glass of sherry?"

"That would be very nice Jonathon," he replied and headed off towards the study. A small light shone on the desk in the study leaving the rest of the room in shadow. He liked it that way. Finding comfort with the darkness that others might not.

As he made himself comfortable on a leather seat behind the desk Veers brought him a glass of sherry on a silver platter. Laying it down on the desk in front of him.

"Would you like anything else sir?"

"Not for now Jonathon but remain awake until I go to bed will you.."

"Yes sir. Your wife called earlier. She asked me to remind you it's Petra's birthday this Saturday."

"As if I'd forget" he replied flatly. His wife, Lady Margaret Cavendish, and he lived separate lives. Her at their estate in Hertfordshire while he remained in London. "Any other calls?"

"None sir," Veers replied.

Cavendish pressed the power button on his laptop, "Bundock has a problem with someone from the past. I do not believe we have to concern ourselves with him finding me, but warn security to be on the alert."

"Of course sir," he said and left him alone.

His attention focused on the laptop as he pressed a thumb print for access. Online he checked a bank account to ensure the £10 million had been lodged. The sound of a key locking the study door loud in the silence. Looking up he was genuinely surprised as Leo Priest lowered himself into a seat opposite crossing his legs pistol in hand.

"I underestimated you," he said.

"People do that," Priest replied.. "You're looking well, but then I guess being such an affluent bloke that's easy." Priest studied the other man's eyes. Older now. Even cosmetic surgery couldn't conceal his age. A short neat grey beard. New nose. Heavier than he remembered too. "Apparently you're quite the business hero these days. Pity I haven't followed business news while in prison otherwise I might have found you earlier."

"I take it Bundock's dead?" He asked.

"Not yet," he replied.

"And what do you hope to achieve by coming here?"

"Do I really need to draw you pictures. I've been thinking about killing you for the past fifteen years."

"Ah, my death. Is that what you really want?" He asked unconvinced.

"You think there's something else?" Priest guessed he would want to play games. Stalling until his security became aware of his presence.

"I could use someone like you. Age has obviously not slowed you down." Cavendish said smoothly as if discussing a potential opening in his organisation rather than struggling to avoid his own demise.

Priest grinned, "You're offering me a job?"

"Why not?"

"You're a murderer for one," he said.

"So are you," Cavendish smiled.

"I was a soldier. Killing enemies to protect this country was what I did."

"Without enjoying it?"

"You're telling me you enjoy killing?"

"Doesn't everyone?" The question of a psychopath. "That momentary sense of power over another. Don't tell me you haven't felt it?"

Priest knew exactly what he meant. Fortunately, in his experience only a small minority found themselves drawn to a need to kill. They're found everywhere living among ordinary people. Psychopaths. The death of others at their hand the ultimate thrill by which some survived the routine burden life throws at us all. Also, escaping capture a part of the thrill. Staying ahead of law enforcement a demonstration of the power they wield. Power over others. "How many have you killed?"

Cavendish caught himself suddenly hesitant. "Of course you'd be working directly for me but ultimately the criminal organization that employs me. They're the ones who really run this gravy train. It was they who helped me have you convicted all those years ago. I suppose if you are angry about your incarceration your grievance is with them maybe even more than me."

"It's you" he replied. "You murdered Michella Baez because she wouldn't let you rape her."

"That's very judgemental of you if you don't mind my saying, considering you were meant to protect me. You failed. You placed me in danger over a silly little girl who meant nothing to anyone."

"Except her parents," he replied. "I watched them during the trial. She meant everything to them. I felt their grief and hatred, which I didn't deserve."

"Good grief man, you're a soldier don't tell me you haven't experienced such things before."

"This was unlike anything I've ever experienced. Undeserved! It meant something different to me too. I've felt troubled by it since the trial." He didn't expect Cavendish to understand. Psychopaths can't stretch their imagination that far. Shameless, uninhibited and without a moral compass they lacked any experience of the values shared by millions. Life was so much simpler for them. Predators have a way of looking at life through a black and white lens denied to the rest of us. He could almost feel envious.

"So, does that mean you're not going to accept my offer?"

"Guess it does." He flatly replied.

"Are you going to kill me?" Cavendish didn't move or show any sign of emotion. Appearing totally calm he seemed ready to die without a plea for mercy.

Priest shrugged, "Maybe."

"What does that mean?" He asked irritated by an answer that held other possibilities.

"You'll find out."

"Just how do you think you're going to get out of here. You heard me talking to Veers. My people are waiting just beyond that door. There's nowhere to go Priest and even if there were do you think the people who employ me will let you get away with anything you do to me?"

"Keeping telling yourself that they bother me if it helps you."

Cavendish chuckled, "You mean that little dead girl means more to you than your own life?"

"You robbed me of fifteen good years and you robbed her of even more. I'm holding you accountable for the both of us."

He lost the humour and glowered back, "You're nothing compared to me Priest. You must be thick if that hasn't sunk in yet!"

"Thick enough to be sitting opposite you with a gun in my hand."

Cavendish appeared to relent, "Haven't you suffered enough because you failed to appreciate my status the first time around. When you die no one is going to care and you'll be lucky to even receive a headline in the press. Whereas anything that happens to me is significant. Powerful people will hunt you down for daring to come after me and anyone stupid enough to help you."

Priest sighed rising from the seat, "Maybe you're right but they might well think twice about it after hearing what Bundock tells them."

"Bundock's as good as dead and he knows it. He broke their code when he identified me that's unforgiveable."

"Agreed, but before he does he will warn them that if they send anyone after me or any of my friends I will come for them. Now get up. We're going up to the roof."

Cavendish rose from the seat, "In movies why do people always run upstairs when trying to escape. I've never understood how they could remotely expect to escape when they can't fly."

"Let's go so you can find out," he said.

Adjusting his jacket Cavendish stepped towards the door Veers had used only for Priest to catch his wrist as he reached for its handle. "Not that way. The bookcase."

"How did you know about that?" He asked genuinely surprised.

"Good intelligence. You lead."

Cavendish strode over to the bookshelves to his left and pressed down on an end book on the third shelf. A click sounded as the shelf swung outwards and lights automatically lit a steep narrow stairway. Veers was alone when he jumped out knife in hand. Striking down hard the blade tore into his shoulder before Priest could move. The pistol in his right hand spat catching Cavendish as he turned. His thigh spitting blood as he hit the floor crying in pain.

Veers face was close as he and Priest rolled to the floor. The smell of garlic on his breath pungent. Briefly more distracting than the knife pressed into his shoulder as Priest fought to lift him away to find a place for the pistol to put a hole in him also. Veers clamped a second hand around the blade and began to twist. The pain agony as it grated against bone. His left hand found Veers throat and pressed into his adam's apple. The other man's eyes suddenly pained as one hand released the blade and struggled to pull his hand free from his neck. It provided a sufficient gap between him and the pistol in Priest's right hand. Before a muffled shot ended their deathly embrace as Veers slumped on top. Pushing the other man off Priest clambered to his feet and pulled out the blade before rushing up the narrow stairs taken by Cavendish. The other man was climbing on his belly almost at the top blood pouring from his leg wound.

"Glad you got this far saved me having to drag you," Priest said.

The other man looked back over his shoulder with unconcealed dismay. "You fool!"

"Keep going."

A hatch at the top of the stairs needed a gentle touch before automatically opening. Climbing out in the centre of a large roof garden with artificial grass and a few genuine potted plants he remained still clutching at his wound as Priest joined him. A blaze of LED lighting lit up the garden leaving no corner in shadow as half a dozen well-armed bodyguards appeared quickly around them.

"I warned you Priest. You're a fool to have thought you could take me. Give yourself up," Cavendish said, looking over his shoulder a smugness in his expression and tone that would ordinarily have prompted a slap from his captor. "If you were hoping for a helicopter rescue look to your right and you'll see one of my men armed with a missile launcher. I'm sure you recognise it. He'll bring down any air support you were hoping to see. Now save us both time as well as the lives of whoever you were expecting by surrendering."

Stealth drones come in all shapes and sizes including features. Incredibly inaudible engines due to their lower weight and size. Remotely controlled from a mobile control unit located in a nearby van provided a powerful air attack system for any military unit with such a need. The three custom built multi-rotor attack drones were half the size of the cargo drones Jacks had previously used. Painted black they were almost invisible at night to the naked eye until too late. While fitted with semi-automatics beneath the rotors they were a 21st century technological weapon that proved both cheap and effective in firefights. As the three drones hovered outside the illuminated area of the roof garden barely making a sound. Their remote operators selected the most dangerous targets and fired. Gun flashes dispelled the darkness in yellows, reds and white bursts that tore into the unsuspecting bodyguards. The stinger anti-aircraft launcher holder one of the first to fall. Moments later only Cavendish and Priest remained standing as a pair of cargo drones emerged from the darkness. One hauling an empty cradle the other with Shimmer and Travis sitting with legs dangling and automatic weapons at the ready. The empty drone came close to where they stood, and Priest nudged Cavendish towards it.

"Climb aboard."

"It doesn't look very safe," he replied unable to disguise the shock of what just happened.

"Better than the alternative," Priest warned.

Stepping onto the ropes he steadied himself while Priest joined him. Moments later the drone lifted into the air with the others following.

# CHAPTER EIGHT

*Accountability*

Sabaneta Prison Maracaibo, Venezuela in South America is said by many to be the most violent and deadly prison in the world. A terrifying place to be accommodated no matter who you were.

That Venezuela is infamous for holding the second highest murder rate in the world. It seems reasonable to expect that Venezuelan prisons be recognised as the most violent anywhere. No less surprising is that even the director of Venezuelan prisons claims that 80% are managed by the armed gangs they're accommodating.

Imagine 3,700 inmates at Sabaneta, the country's most violent being packed into accommodation designed for just 700 and you get an idea why death is considered a very positive solution to improve personal space. Particularly as filth and neglect rank high while a guard rate ratio of 150:1 is insufficient to do more than observe.

When Lord Cavendish slipped quietly amongst the other prisoners any thought of complaining dissolved as the stench of human excrement and overheated bodies welcomed him. Together with the dull hostile gazes from each prisoner moving aside for him.

In Venezuela anything can be bought for the right price. Having Cavendish incarcerated for life without any possibility of his former employers or indeed the British government                locating                him                cost

Bs286,434,107,816,982,496.00 bolivars or £1,000,000 pounds sterling. It also bought a more than reluctant silence from the man himself after being warned that any attempt to identify himself would cause his tongue to be cut out. Seeing the once arrogant merciless murderer reduced to tearful fear gave Priest a little surprising satisfaction.

Watching him move among the prison crowd taking their daily exercise in a yard for 700 packed with 3700 was something else to behold. As he moved further among them, so he quickly became lost like a fish mixed into a school.

Beside him Jacks sighed, the overbearing summer heat making him hot. "His bosses are going to know it was us."

"Inevitably," Priest agreed.

"D'you think they'll come?"

"Possibly, but they'll know if they don't get it right first time they'd have opened a can of worms."

"Good job none of us wants to die old then."

"The price for accountability."

## THE END

**NOTES:** For the purposes of this fiction novel Sabaneta prison is used though it has been closed for some time. Please see the details below: **The Maracaibo National Prison**, also known as Sabaneta Prison, was a notoriously violent prison located in the city of Maracaibo, Venezuela, in the state of Zulia. Let me provide some details: The prison closed in 2013 after a riot that resulted in the deaths of sixteen inmates. Overcrowding and violence at the root cause of the riots. Like many Venezuelan prisons, Sabaneta suffered from severe overcrowding, inadequate access to medical care, food, and clean water. Violence among prisoners was common, and gangs controlled the prison, led by an "inmate leader" known as a "pran".

The prison population was originally built to accommodate 700 prisoners, but by 2013 this had risen to 3,700 inmates, including an estimated 192 children of the inmates.

The prison was structured into four main areas:

**Procemil**: For military officers and police agents

**Re-education**: For criminals with light sentences

**Prison:** Containing a variety of standard prisoners

**Maximum**: For prisoners with the most serious charges

**Notable Incidents** 1994 Riot & Fire: A deadly riot erupted in the prison due to gang activity. Inmates started a fire and many were killed during the chaos. Security personnel's attempts to regain control resulted in additional casualties. Other Riots: Smaller riots occurred regularly, often attributed to gang violence among prisoners. In 2013 alone 69 prisoners were killed. Closure and

**Future Plans**: The prison was closed after 55 years of operation due to government intervention. Currently, there are no plans to reopen it as a museum, allowing citizens to visit the sites of famous massacres and learn about the historical operation of corrupt prison systems.

In August 2023, there were reports that local residents feared the Sabaneta prison had reopened, but this information remains unverified.

Sabaneta Prison

## ACCOUNTABILITY TWO

There are plans to follow-up Accountability with a second novel that will have Leo Priest and Puss-in-Boots again engaged in activities they are forced to confront. Expect the second book to be available in 2025.

Other Books by this author on Amazon

**Memory Loss**

Having all his memories artificially removed investigative journalist Vernon Bass finds himself confronted by an unfamiliar emptiness.

He is first discovered in Italy, on a track that circles a mountain and is rescued and taken to a nearby hospital. His reaction to the artificial treatment that took his memories fails to prevent muscle memories from returning together with heartfelt memories of his childhood until eventually only the past five years remain lost to him.

As he strives to find what he has lost he accepts an offer to trial a machine that may return his lost memories. What happens then is nothing his doctors had ever envisaged.

## Space Village One

Escaping an abusive partner is as tough in 2060 as it was in 2020. You just have further to run.

Melissa is on the run from her controlling husband, the Prime minister of the British Democratic Republic.

Her escape plan includes a trip to Space Village One where she believes she can ask for sanctuary. With tensions growing between countries on the surface the leader of Space Village One has difficult decision to make.

## The Satanic Chapel

Detective Chief Inspector Betty Buick and her team of detectives encounter a supernatural cult that believes it is able to control the Devil himself.

As unexplained deaths mount and detectives stationed elsewhere go missing the Commissioner of the Metropolitan Police turns to Buick to find answers.

Little does Buick realise that her life will be changed forever when she finally meets the most wicked of foes.

## The White Coven Belfast

Three sisters living in Belfast operate as the primary defence against evil in Ireland.

Much older than their looks they are descended from ancient witches who have kept humanity from falling into the foul hands of the Devil.

They are again called to defend humanity as the forces of darkness infest the small island with its disciples.

### They're Having A Laugh!

Athe first in a series of political satire involving Prime
Minister Rupert Streaker

British Prime Minister Rupert Streaker finds himself on the front
pages of every daily for the wrong reasons. Rumours of an extra-
marital affair with a childhood sweetheart bad enough. Lurid
photographs of an erotic encounter in a church during university
days shatter his peace both at home and on the work fronts.
Saving his career as well as his marriage now the focus of
attention. Can he save both or will no amount of spin be enough?
In an alternative reality, anything can happen